MW00596618

TILL DEATH DO US PART

EVA RAE THOMAS MYSTERY - BOOK 14

WILLOW ROSE

What's coming next from Willow Rose?

Get on the list to find out about coming titles, bargains, giveaways, and more.
WILLOW ROSE VIP NEWSLETTER.
Go here to sign up: https://readerlinks.com/l/415254

Marriage is the most natural state of man, and the state in which you will find solid happiness.

- Benjamin Franklin

He who finds a wife, finds a good thing and obtains favor from the Lord.

Proverbs 18:22

Prologue

Monday morning

COCOA BEACH, Florida

Chapter 1

It was a Monday morning like so many others. Rachel and John Baker were both late getting out the door. Their eight-year-old son Thomas barely made it out in time for the school bus. The twins, Robert and Maria, were crying helplessly as they got them dressed and rushed them out the door, off to daycare. John and Rachel were fighting all the way there in the car, and they finally arrived at the daycare, flustered and exasperated.

"Can you take the diaper bag?" Rachel asked, grabbing Robert in her arms.

John sighed, annoyed, and grabbed the bag and Maria then slammed the car door.

"It's not like it's a lot to ask," Rachel said.

"Why can't you take the darn bag then?" he asked.

She sighed in annoyance, then grabbed the bag and pulled it from his hand. She walked with determined steps toward the entrance, wishing things were different between them.

It hadn't always been like this. Once upon a time, they were the perfect couple, but now it felt like they were living in two different worlds. How had this happened to them?

They barely made it inside the preschool's tall building before both twins started crying helplessly. Robert clung to his mother and wouldn't let go. Rachel wanted to scream herself. It was the same every morning, and she hated it so much.

"It's okay, honey. Mommy will pick you up this afternoon after your nap, okay?"

But Robert wouldn't calm down, and his sister cried along with him just as loudly. Many of the other parents looked at them, and Rachel felt embarrassed.

She was the one who had wanted them to go to daycare. She wanted to go back to work; she loved it, but John wanted her to stay at home.

"Shh, shh," she said, caressing Robert's hair gently while rocking him, praying he would stop soon.

Suddenly, Maria started crying even louder, and Rachel realized she had forgotten the pacifier in the car. She handed Robert to John and rushed out to get it. When she came back, she saw him deep in conversation with a gorgeous woman who looked to be ten years younger than Rachel. And worst of all, he was paying no attention to his crying children, completely ignoring them.

What the heck?

The woman was giggling and playing with her hair. Rachel couldn't help but feel insecure as she noticed the way the woman was looking at John. She knew that look all too well—and especially the way he looked at her.

Oh, no, not again!

Rachel's heart pounded as she approached them, trying to maintain her composure.

"What's going on here?" she asked, trying to sound calm.

John turned to her, surprised. "Oh, hey, Rachel. This is Emily; we were just talking. She works at the art gallery across the street from my office."

Emily smiled at Rachel. It was friendly but guarded. "Hi, nice to meet you."

She knew the look John was giving Emily—the same look he used to give her when they first met. The same look he had given his old assistant when they had an affair, and Rachel had left him until he promised he would fire her and never see her again. She had seen it countless times before and knew exactly where this was heading.

Rachel forced a smile, but inside, she was seething. "Nice to meet you, too. John, can we go now? The twins are still crying."

John nodded, handing Robert back to Rachel. "Sure." He turned to Emily.

"Maybe we can continue this conversation later?"

"Sure, I'd like that," Emily said, batting her eyelashes.

Rachel felt a whiplash of jealousy. The audacity he had to flirt with this woman right in front of her. Who did he think he was? She couldn't shake off the feeling that something was going on between them. But she didn't want to make a scene in front of the other parents, so she kept her cool. As they walked out of the daycare, Rachel couldn't help but feel helpless and lost. She didn't know what to do. She didn't want to confront John about it because he would just deny anything was going on and tell her more lies like last time. But she couldn't just ignore it either.

Once they were in the car, John started the engine and turned to Rachel. It was only a three-minute drive to John's work at the real estate office, where she would drop him off and then head to the hospital where she worked as a nurse practitioner.

"What's wrong?" he asked.

"Nothing," Rachel lied, avoiding eye contact. Rachel was trying to hold back her tears. She couldn't believe that John was flirting with another woman right in front of her. She knew she had to confront him about it, but she didn't know how to start.

John sighed. "Look, I know we've been having some problems

lately, but I promise you... nothing is going on between Emily and me."

Rachel scoffed. "Right, just like nothing was going on between you and your former assistant?"

"That was a long time ago, Rachel. I thought we had moved past that."

Rachel rolled her eyes. "How can I be sure you're telling the truth?"

John reached over and took her hand. "You just have to trust me. I love you, Rachel. You're the only one for me."

Rachel wanted to believe him; she really, really did.

Chapter 2

Kyla was sitting at the kitchen table, mindlessly scrolling through her phone, when suddenly her mother called. She sighed since she wasn't really in the mood to talk to her right now, but she also knew if she didn't pick up, her mother would be nervous and keep calling until she did pick up. Her mother was relentless when it came to those sorts of things. She knew her children's schedules and that Kyla wasn't working today. She exhaled, steadying herself, then picked it up. Barely had she said hi when she heard the sound of her mother's voice.

"Have you heard from your sister?"

Kyla shook her head. Now, it was her sister Rachel she was worried about. There was always something. "No, well... not since this morning. I sent her a funny picture around 8:15, and she sent something back, something silly really, but I haven't heard anything since then."

Kyla's mother sighed heavily. "That's what I was afraid of," she said. "I've called some of her friends and John, and none of them have heard from her either. I'm worried something might have happened."

Kyla chuckled. Her mother always overreacted to these sorts of things. If she didn't hear back from her daughters immediately, she always thought they were dead in a ditch somewhere. She didn't understand that they were busy people with busy lives and couldn't always answer anytime she needed them to.

"I'm sure she's fine," she said. "She had to work today. She's probably just too busy to answer. You know how it is."

"I'm not sure," she said. "This feels different."

"You always say that," Kyla said.

"No, this time really is different," she said. "We were supposed to babysit tonight, and she hasn't even told us what time. When I text her, she doesn't answer. I even tried calling, but it went to voicemail. I also called the hospital, and she didn't come in for work today."

Kyla felt a chill run down her spine. Rachel always made it to work. She never stayed home or took a day off. She usually told them everything she was doing, but today, she hadn't said anything since that silly picture of the cat and the gorilla she had sent her this morning. Kyla tried to think positively, but the fear kept creeping in.

"Maybe she's just busy," she said again. "It doesn't have to be anything serious. Maybe her phone just died, and she couldn't find anywhere to charge it?"

Her mother exhaled. "Maybe," she said pensively. "But I'm not comfortable with this. At all. Why isn't she at work? She's always there."

"I'll try and call around as well," Kyla said, mostly to comfort her mother. She still felt confident that there was a reasonable explanation for Rachel's silence. After all, it had only been a few hours that she hadn't been responding. She was entitled to some privacy if she needed it.

Kyla hung up, feeling helpless. She wished there was something she could do, but she knew there wasn't. All she could do was wait for Rachel to call and hope she was safe.

Kyla spent the next few hours anxiously waiting for that very call from her sister. She tried calling her a few times, but it went straight to voicemail each time. She checked all her social media accounts, but there was no activity on any of them. She even tried calling some of Rachel's friends, but none of them had heard from her either. The more time that passed, the more worried Kyla became.

As the sun began to set, Kyla's phone finally rang. She jumped to answer it, hoping it was Rachel. But it wasn't. It was a police officer. Kyla's heart raced as she listened to the officer on the other end of the line.

"We found your sister's car abandoned on the side of the road, the door left open, the car still running," the officer said. "We've been searching the area, but we haven't been able to locate her or anyone else who might have been operating the vehicle. We found her phone inside the car, and she has this number listed as her ICE (in case of emergency). We also found her wallet in the car with her driver's license. We're worried about what could have happened here. Have you heard from her?"

"N-no. Not since this morning."

"That's odd," he said. "Is she suffering from any sort of mental health problems? Could she have just walked off? Has this happened before?"

"N-no, no, mental health issues. She takes Prozac for depression, but that's not out of the...."

"Could she have tried to hurt herself?"

"She's not suicidal if that's what you're asking."

"Okay. We'll treat this as a missing person's case. We need you to come down to the station and give us all the information you have on your sister," the officer said. "We'll also need you to make a formal statement."

Kyla numbly agreed and hung up the phone. She felt like she was in a daze as she gathered her things and made her way to the police station. As she drove, her mind raced with thoughts of her sister. Where could she be? Was she hurt? Was she scared?

Kyla's world felt like it had crumbled around her. She couldn't believe this was happening. Her sister, missing? This couldn't be true. She had asked the officer for more details, but he didn't have any. They were still searching the area and investigating the situation.

Kyla felt tears streaming down her face. She couldn't even imagine what her mother would go through. She knew she had to call and tell her the news, but she didn't know how. How could she tell her that her daughter was missing?

Eventually, Kyla mustered up the strength to call her mother. She parked the car in front of the police station, about to walk in, then made the call. She could barely get the words out. Her mother was hysterical on the other end of the line. Kyla did her best to comfort her but felt just as lost as her mother. She hung up and walked into the station. She wondered why Rachel had put her as her emergency contact instead of her husband but then shook the thought.

KYLA STARED AT HER FINGERS, then bit her nails nervously while looking around at the police station. She was sitting by the detective's desk and had just been giving him all the information on her sister. Kyla had been there for what felt like an eternity, her mind spinning in a billion different directions as she wondered where her sister could have gone and why no one had seen her.

It felt like a bad dream, a nightmare.

Suddenly, there was a commotion outside the door, and it was flung open. A tall, flustered figure stood in the doorway, his face scrunched up with worry and anger as he looked around wildly.

John.

"What's going on here? Where is my wife?" he demanded.

Kyla got to her feet slowly, something strange blooming in her chest. There was something off about how he behaved; he seemed too agitated and anxious. From the start, she couldn't help but wonder if he was somehow involved in her sister's disappearance.

She wouldn't put it past him.

John continued to bark out more questions, but the detective intervened before Kyla could say anything.

"Sir, we don't know where your wife is," he said calmly. "But we'll do our best to find her. Please take a seat, and we'll let you know if there are any updates."

John grudgingly obeyed, and Kyla returned to her seat, her gaze still locked on John, feeling oddly suspicious of him. Something told her that he knew more than he was willing to admit.

As Kyla sat there staring at John, she couldn't help but feel a sense of dread wash over her. There was something in his eyes that made her skin crawl. She watched as he fidgeted in his seat and clenched his fists tightly, his jaw set in a hard line. Kyla couldn't shake off the feeling that something was wrong. She had known her sister and John's relationship had been rocky lately, but she never thought it would lead to something like this.

What did you do to her, you bastard?

The longer she stared at him, the more convinced she became that he was hiding something. She had never liked John and always thought he was too controlling and possessive of her sister. She was barely allowed to go out with her friends, let alone her sister. He was scared she might find someone else. And then he ended up being the one who had an affair, the fool—as if Rachel didn't have enough to do with those three children that John never took care of. Rachel had chosen to forgive him, but it had been hard on their marriage. He was an idiot and not good enough for Rachel. She deserved way more.

15

Kyla had warned her when they first met—told her this would end badly. But her sister wouldn't listen. Of course not. Once she had told Kyla that she was pregnant for the first time, Kyla knew there was no way they'd ever get rid of him. He was family now. He and Kyla often argued at dinners at their mother's, and she believed he was being rude to their mother as he showed her no respect. He always had that look in his eyes like he was guilty of something—like he had done something wrong and was only waiting for the world to find out who he really was. But this was different. There was an intensity in his gaze that she had never seen before, and it made her heart race with unease.

Suddenly, John stood up and strode over to Kyla, his face just inches from hers.

"What do you know?" he growled, his breath hot against her face. "What have you done with her?"

Kyla recoiled, her heart pounding in her chest.

"I don't know what you're talking about," she stammered. "I want to ask you the same thing."

John's eyes narrowed, and he took a step closer, his hand clenching into a fist. "Don't lie to me," he hissed. "I know you've always hated me. I bet you're behind all of this. You probably convinced Rachel to leave me and run away, right?"

Kyla's eyes widened in disbelief and fear. Was he serious? How could he even think that?

"I would never do something like that!" she protested, stepping back. "I love my sister! I want her to come back just as much as you do!"

John sneered at her.

"Sure, you do," he said sarcastically. "You've always been jealous of our relationship. You've always wanted to tear us apart. Don't think I haven't noticed how you always talk bad about me when I'm not there."

Kyla shook her head in disbelief. "Yeah, well, that isn't too often these days, is it? You follow her around and listen in on all her conversations. Don't think I haven't noticed. You're crazy," she said.

John's expression darkened, and he grabbed her by the wrist, pulling her toward him. "Don't you dare call me crazy!"

John's eyes narrowed dangerously as he tightened his grip on Kyla's arm, causing her to flinch in pain.

"Don't you dare lie to me," John hissed. "I know you've always despised me. You're probably enjoying this, aren't you? My wife disappears, and suddenly, everyone's pointing fingers at me."

Kyla tried to pull away from him. "Let go of me," she demanded, her voice shaking with fear and anger. "You have no right to touch me."

The detective got up and signaled for help to a couple of officers. They reacted and approached them.

John smirked as they grabbed him and pulled him away from her. "I have every right. I'm her husband. It's my job to protect her."

Kyla stumbled back, startled, her eyes flashing with fury.

"Protect her?" she spat. "The way you protected her when you cheated on her? Or when you constantly belittled her and made her feel worthless?

John's face reddened with anger, but Kyla didn't back down. "You have no right to accuse me of anything. You're the one who has something to hide. Where were you when she disappeared?"

John's expression hardened as they held him and told him to please calm down. "You think you're so clever, don't you?" he snarled. "You think you can just accuse me of something and get away with it?"

Kyla stood her ground, refusing to back down. "I'm not accusing you of anything," she said firmly. "I just know that something isn't right here. Rachel wouldn't just disappear like this. You have to know something."

John's eyes narrowed, and he finally stopped fighting the officers. They let him go, and he sat down. As the uniformed officers stepped aside, he yelled:

"You want to know what I know?" he growled, again getting to his feet. "I know that you're a liar. I know that you're jealous of our relationship. I know that you're the one who did this."

"Sir, I'm gonna need you to calm down now," the detective said. "Sit down, sir."

For a moment, John seemed to hesitate, his eyes flickering between Kyla and the two police officers watching them both warily. Then, he turned on his heel and stormed out of the station, slamming the door behind him.

Kyla stood there for a moment, her heart racing with adrenaline and fear. She knew that John wasn't telling her everything and that he was somehow involved in her sister's disappearance. But she didn't know how to prove it or what to do next.

She turned to the detective, who was watching her with a mix of concern and suspicion.

"What happens now?" she asked.

The detective took a deep breath, then exhaled slowly.

"We'll continue our investigation," he said finally. "We'll interview anyone who may have seen or heard something and follow up on any leads we get. But I have to be honest with you, Ms. Johnson. In cases like this, the first few hours and days are critical. The longer Rachel is missing, the harder it becomes to find her."

Kyla felt a lump form in her throat. She couldn't bear the thought of her sister being out there somewhere, alone and scared. She had to do something. She had to find her.

"I want to help," she said firmly. "I want to do whatever I can to find her."

Part I

WEDNESDAY

Chapter 1

"Ha, I knew I could do it!"

I looked at my work, hands at my sides, a satisfied smile on my face. It wasn't half bad if I had to say so myself—not perfect, but good enough.

I had just finished laying the wood flooring for Elijah's bedroom when the phone began to ring. Matt and I had decided to try to do as many of the renovations on the house as we could ourselves to save money, and I was surprised at how well we were doing so far. Annoyed at the phone ringing, I stopped staring at my work. Crouching, sweat dripping from my forehead, I looked up at Matt, who was putting the final coat of paint on the walls, and nodded toward the phone. He nodded back but kept his attention on the task at hand.

I scrambled up and hurried to answer the phone, already knowing who it was: my boss, the Chief of the Cocoa Beach Police Department.

"Eva Rae," she said in her no-nonsense voice, "we've got a strange case of a missing thirty-six-year-old woman. Something about her disappearance doesn't add up, and I need your help to investigate. We can't figure out what is up and what is down. She's been gone for forty-eight hours now, and still no sign of her. I'm worried. She has three children. It has turned into a custody battle now since the sister doesn't want the dad around the children, claiming he has hurt the wife, and he might hurt them too."

My heart skipped a beat. When children were involved, you didn't need to ask me twice.

"What can I do?" I asked breathlessly.

"Come down to the station as soon as you can," she said. "We need to get to the bottom of this. Bring Matt. We need the both of you."

I hung up the phone and told Matt about the urgent phone call. He nodded gravely and, without a word, stopped what he was doing, putting down the brush. I quickly put on my shoes and picked up my purse, and together, we drove to the police station.

As soon as we arrived, we were ushered into a small conference room where Chief Annie and two other detectives were waiting for us. Annie was a tall, intimidating woman with a no-nonsense attitude. She motioned for us to sit down and began briefing us on the details of the case.

"Thanks for coming, Eva Rae, Matt," Chief Annie said as she stood up to greet us. "Our missing person's case is a bit of a puzzle. The missing woman's name is Rachel Baker."

I looked up at the chief with a small gasp. I knew this woman, or rather, I knew her son, Thomas, as he was in the same grade at Roosevelt Elementary as my son, Alex. Alex loved Thomas, and they played so well together that I often had the boy over for playdates. I often invited Rachel in for a glass of wine or coffee when she came to pick him up, and I enjoyed her company. This news made me feel sick to my stomach.

"She's a mother of three," Chief Annie continued, "and she

was last seen dropping off her twins at FUMC daycare on A1A with her husband at eight o'clock in the morning. She texted her sister at eight-fifteen—some silly cat picture and her sister texted her back. This was right before she left the daycare area. She was supposed to go to work that day as a nurse practitioner at Cape Canaveral Hospital, but she never showed up. A patrol found her car abandoned on the side of the road by the Air Force station at one-thirteen p.m., and that's the last sign of life."

"At the Air Force station? But that's in the opposite direction of the hospital," I said. "You said she was going to work, right? From the daycare center?"

Chief Annie nodded. "Exactly. That's one of the things that puzzles us. She was supposed to drop off her husband at Sunshine Real Estate downtown and then head to work. He showed up at work right after nine o'clock, which gives us forty-five minutes to an hour that he's unaccounted for—from when he helps drop off the children until he makes it in for work. We've searched the entire area where the car was found, but there's no sign of her. Her car was parked where we believe she left it, abandoned on the side of the road. Her phone and purse were left in the car. It's like she vanished into thin air."

Matt and I exchanged glances, knowing what we had to do. We asked the chief for more details about the woman and her family, and she gave us a file with all the information they had gathered so far. We looked through the file, trying to piece together any clues that could lead us to Rachel Baker. Her family background was pretty normal, with no signs of criminal activity or history. It seemed like she was leading an everyday life—if there ever was such a thing—with a loving husband and three young children.

"Where do we begin?" Matt said, running a hand through his hair. He still had some paint in it and on his hands, too. I realized I had splinters in my fingers from laying the wooden floors, and my hands were very dirty.

"We need to talk to the husband," I said, looking into his eyes. "But first, I think we need to shower."

Chapter 2

THEN:

They could be punished for everything and nothing. They never knew when it would hit. The girls, living alone with their mother in the townhome, always tried their best to please her, but even their best simply wasn't enough.

Emma first realized it when she was six years old, and her mother entered her room to check if she had cleaned it.

Emma sat on the edge of her bed, clutching her teddy bear tightly. Her mother's eyes scanned the room, taking in every detail with a critical eye. She held her breath, sensing that something wasn't right. Her mother scrutinized everything in the room, from the toys on the floor to the neatly made bed.

"Your bed isn't made properly," her mother said, her voice cold and sharp.

Emma's heart sank. She had spent so much time trying to make her bed look perfect, but apparently, it wasn't good enough.

"I'm sorry, Mommy," Emma whispered, tears welling in her eyes.

Her mother's expression softened slightly, but only for a moment.

"You need to learn to do things right, Emma," she said. "Otherwise, you'll end up a failure. No children of mine will be raised to be failures."

The words stung like a physical blow, and Emma buried her face in her teddy bear, trying to block out the sound of her mother's voice.

When her mother's eyes landed on the teddy bear in her hands, she pulled it from her and examined it closely.

"What is this doing here?" she asked, her voice sharp with anger. "Why isn't it on the shelf?"

Emma's heart raced as she struggled to find an answer. "I-I don't know," she stammered, her eyes downcast.

"You don't know?" her mother repeated, her tone incredulous. That's when it happened. That was the first time Emma remembered seeing those dark eyes in her mother's face. It was like her entire face changed, and a dark curtain was pulled in front of her eyes until they turned black.

Her mother threw the teddy bear on the floor in a fit of rage, and Emma huddled in the corner. She then opened each and every drawer and emptied out her clothes, grabbed the boxes with toys and poured them all onto the floor, then left it all scattered in her room. Then she grabbed Emma by the arm and yanked her up from the bed.

"You call this clean, you little brat?" she hissed, her face contorted with rage. Emma tried to explain that she had been playing with the teddy bear, and that's why it was in her hand, but her mother wasn't listening. She looked at her watch, then at Emma and her two-year-younger sister Lily, whom she shared the room with and who hadn't helped clean up anything at all, only made it all worse.

Emma's mom got in her face and hissed.

"I'm giving you an hour to clean up this mess. Do you hear me? I don't want to see as much as one toy or even a speck of dust anywhere. Do you hear me?"

Emma looked at her feet with a sniffle, then nodded. "Y-yes, Mommy."

"So, what do you say to me?"

She looked up, not knowing what she meant.

"Yes, I will clean up."

She got in the girl's face again. "I want you to say you're sorry. Come on, let me hear it."

Emma bit back tears. She knew it would only make it worse if she began to cry.

"SAY IT!"

"S-sorry," she said, shaking.

Her mother stood up straight. "That's better. Now, promise me you'll be a good girl from now on. I want you perfect."

Emma could barely speak. "I-I'll be a good girl. I promise."

Her mother's nostrils were flaring, and Emma wasn't sure what she had said was enough.

"I promise to be better, Mommy," she said, bursting into tears.

"Okay. Now get to work. If it's not clean in an hour, you're scrubbing the kitchen floor, you hear me?"

"Y-yes, Mommy."

Chapter 3

As we pulled up to the house, now both of us clean and smelling better, the husband, John, was outside, working on his truck. He stiffened as he saw us and seemed to pause for a moment before continuing his work under the hood. It seemed like an odd thing to do when your wife was missing, but maybe that was just me.

"John Baker?"

He looked up, then wiped his wrench on a towel.

John Baker stood motionless as he stared at us. He was a man of medium build with a receding hairline. His pale blue eyes locked onto ours. The wrench in his hand glistened with oil, and the smell of gasoline hung thick in the air. His truck's engine was still running with a low rumble.

John wore an expression of surprise, yet his face remained unreadable. There was an inexplicable sense of detachment emanating from him as if the only thing keeping him from crumbling into a million pieces was his own indomitable will.

"John Baker?" I repeated, my voice cutting through the silence.

He paused for a moment before wordlessly nodding in response. After a few seconds, he finally spoke.

"Yes?"

"I'm FBI Agent Eva Rae Thomas, and this is Detective Matt Miller. We would like to talk to you about your wife, Rachel."

John's face fell, and his gaze shifted away from ours. He seemed to be lost in thought, so I continued.

"We understand if this is a difficult time for you, but we need your help."

Finally, John looked up and met my gaze. His expression softened, and he nodded his head in agreement.

"What can I do?" he said in a low voice. "I've already told them everything down at the station."

"We know this, Mr. Baker, but we're here with some follow-up questions if that's okay with you."

He nodded. "Of course."

Matt stepped forward. "We were told that you had almost an hour unaccounted for on the morning when she disappeared between eight and nine a.m. You dropped off the children together at the daycare center at eight but didn't show up at work until nine o'clock. Where were you?"

John paused again before answering as if carefully considering his words. "I was just... walking," he said, averting his gaze and picking up another tool. "Just clearing my head, you know? I've had a lot going on lately."

I glanced at Matt, who gave me a subtle nod. We both knew what the other was thinking... that John was hiding something. It didn't take an expert to know this.

"Did you take a walk with someone who can confirm that's what you did?"

He shook his head. "Nope."

"Okay, were you with anyone who can confirm where you were? Did you meet anyone on your way? Where did you go?"

He shrugged. "I just went down to the beach. I didn't have any meetings until ten, so I thought I had some time to wind down, you know? Having toddlers is a lot, and sometimes, I need to go down to the ocean and just breathe."

Having four children myself, I knew what he was saying. I couldn't hold that against him. Heck, I still needed a break now and then, especially from the teenagers and all their breakdowns. They were often worse than the toddlers.

"So, you didn't talk to anyone or...?" I asked.

He shook his head. "Nope."

"Have you seen any cars around here, any suspicious activity, or maybe someone keeping an eye on the house? Anyone new calling you?"

"Nope."

He paused, then looked at me. "Come to think of it, yes. Rachel often got these calls—sometimes, in the middle of the night. It said no caller ID on them, and no one was there the few times she picked up. We thought it was just the usual scam, you know?"

"I've been getting a lot of that, too," Matt said.

"But not in the middle of the night. We should try and get her phone records from the provider," I told him.

"Of course."

"Is it possible she could have left?" I asked.

John closed the truck's hood, then wiped sweat off his forehead. "That's what I'm afraid of," he said. "We haven't been doing great lately, and I'm afraid she just took off."

"Would that be something she might do?" I asked.

He mulled it over for a few seconds. "I... I don't know if I'm being honest. She loved her children so much, but still. She was sick of us and of this whole situation. Especially of me. Maybe."

"Her family, her mother and sister in particular, seem to believe a crime has been committed. Do you agree?"

He shrugged. "Not really. At first, yes. But then I came back home, and I went on her computer and found out she had been searching for plane tickets, so if I'm honest, I fear she just left me. It pisses me off, of course, because we have children together, and I love her, even if I haven't been the best at showing it to her. We're still married; you don't just run off from that. It's supposed to be till death do you part and all that. You don't just take off and leave just because it gets a little hard, you know?"

I nodded in agreement. "You said she searched for plane tickets? Where to?"

"New York," he said. "She used to live up there before we were married."

I wrote it down.

"Was she looking to fly out of Orlando?"

"Yes."

I made a note of it and reminded myself to have it checked if she appeared on any flights recently.

"She was depressed, I understand? She took medication for her depression. Maybe she thought it was too much?"

He nodded. "That's what I'm thinking. I keep hoping she will come home any day now and say she's sorry and just needed to blow off some steam. That's kind of what I'm hoping for."

"That makes sense. Would you say she could be suicidal, though?" I asked.

He exhaled and rubbed the sweat off his forehead. "I have never heard her mention anything about that, no. But you never know with people, right? They always say that the ones who do kill themselves are the ones who never talk about it, right? She could be."

"Could we see the computer and the search for the plane tickets, please?" I asked.

He nodded and wiped his fingers.

"Yes, of course. Follow me."

Chapter 4

Kyla heard the sound of crunching gravel and squealing tires and looked outside just in time to see her mother drive into her driveway.

Uh-oh. Now what?

She barely put her wine glass down before her mother burst through the door. Her hair was disheveled, and her clothes were rumpled with sweat as if she had been running for miles. There were tears in her eyes, and her voice trembled when she spoke.

"Kyla!" she shouted, desperation growing with every word. "Have you heard anything? Any news?"

Kyla was taken aback; she didn't like to see such a panicked reaction from her mother. She wanted to calm her down—make her feel better.

"Not yet, Mom. I'm sure they're working on it, though," she said.

"Sure? That's not enough!"

"Well, it's all I got."

Kyla had been worried all day and constantly looking at her

phone to see if she had missed a call from the police or maybe even Rachel herself. It most certainly wasn't like Rachel not to keep them updated on where she was or what she was doing. It was very concerning, and now that the day was almost over, she was not feeling too great and had opened a bottle of wine to calm her nerves. Kyla loved her sister so deeply, and they had always been very close. This wasn't good, and they both knew it—both her and their mom.

Her mother's expression shifted from fear to anger as she looked at Kyla, almost like she blamed her for her sister's disappearance.

"We have to do something!" she said.

"What do you want me to do?" Kyla asked.

Her mom threw out her arms. "I don't know. Think of something!"

"I know the police have search parties out there, and John and I were part of one earlier today. We went through the entire area out by the Air Force base and the beach, the entire neighborhood where the car was found."

Her mother crept closer and pointed a finger at her. "He's done something. I just know it. I've never liked him. I'm telling ya'. I knew this would happen one day. I just knew it, but would she listen? Oh, no."

Kyla sighed. "That's what I keep telling the police. But when they don't have a body, it's hard for them to know if there has been an actual crime."

"Oh, don't even say that, " her mother said and clasped her chest. "Don't joke about such things. "

"Yeah, okay, but it's the truth. She is a grown woman who could just have left her husband and children. It happens. "

"That's nonsense, " her mother hissed. "Rachel would never do that. "

"You're preaching to the choir."

"I don't like that the children are with him," she said. "What if he hurts them too?"

"Again, I have literally told that to the police."

"I hear about stories like that all the time on the news, where some father kills his entire family. We can't let that happen to them. Do you hear me?"

"Yes, Mom. I agree."

Kyla felt like someone had plunged a knife into her heart. She felt so worried for her poor sister.

"I just know something happened to her," her mother said, her fists clenching in rage. "The police don't seem to be doing anything. We have to do something. We have to find Rachel and make sure she's safe—and the children, of course. They're our priority now."

"I will talk to a lawyer tomorrow," Kyla said.

"I know a good one," her mom said, grabbing her phone. "I'll text you his info. He can help us."

Chapter 5

Matt and I sat at the dinner table in exhausted silence. The children had gone to their rooms, Angel had been put down for the night, and the dishes had been put away. The day had been full of investigation and questioning, but the seriousness of the case still lingered in the air like an electric current. We both knew that all we wanted was to collapse into bed and take solace in the darkness of sleep, but neither of us could bring ourselves to move. The adrenaline was still rushing through our bodies. Matt tapped his fingers on the dining room table; the sound was like a drummer's cymbals, a staccato beat of percussion instruments.

We were both so lost in thought that we jumped when my telephone suddenly rang, the shrill sound shattering the room's stillness. I hurried to it, my heart pounding, and picked it up.

"Yes?" I said, my voice tense.

On the other end of the line was a voice I recognized. It was the chief, and she had news. I put the call on speakerphone so Matt could listen in.

"The airline confirms that Rachel bought tickets to fly to New

York on the day she disappeared. The flight left at 12:15 but without her. She checked in online but never showed up at the airport," Annie, the Chief of Police, said. There was a long silence as Matt and I processed this information.

"So, what does this mean?" I finally asked. "Could she still be in town?"

"It's possible," Annie replied. "But it looks like she might have attempted to leave town without telling anyone." She paused momentarily before adding, "But why she never showed up... that's the mystery. We'll have to look into that. It worries me."

My pulse raced as we hung up, and I turned to Matt and saw the same anticipation in his eyes.

"So, we have the plane tickets for New York," I said and grabbed the wine, then poured myself another glass. I handed him a beer from the fridge, throwing a glance around me. The house was a mess since we were still renovating the kitchen and the extra rooms upstairs. Elijah's room was only half painted, and we still needed to put the new toilet in the bathroom. I sort of wanted to get it done right away, but I simply couldn't. I could see on Matt's face that neither could he. We had no more energy for today, and it would have to wait. I couldn't even stand to look at my kitchen and hadn't been able to cook as it was such a mess. We had ordered Thai food instead, which the children had been very happy about.

"But the airline says she never showed up. She checked in that very morning online, so she was planning on going, we must assume, and her husband didn't know of it. What the heck happened to her?"

Matt nodded. "Okay, so here's my theory. What if John found out about the tickets earlier? What if he didn't just see them today? He could have found them days or maybe even weeks ago and just not told her."

"Yeah," I said and sipped my wine pensively. "I was thinking the same thing. You think he got angry? Realizing she was planning on leaving him?"

Matt nodded and drank from his beer. "Exactly. Could it be that she was trying to leave, and then John killed her because he didn't want her to leave him?" he said, his voice somber.

"It's definitely a possibility and a motive. But what did he do to her if he did? We don't know if she's still out there somewhere. She might be alive."

Matt sighed. "Or maybe she found another way of leaving—one John couldn't track. Did she have any money? Maybe stored away in a secret account somewhere? Did she have friends in the area? Maybe some that John didn't know about? Where he wouldn't come looking for her?"

I shook my head. There was a lot of work to be done. I was just hoping I could sleep and wouldn't lie awake thinking about this. I tended to keep mulling things over and over in my mind instead of sleeping.

"We need to find that out. We still need to look into her finances more, see if there's any indication of her leaving in a more mysterious fashion." I sighed, leaning back in my chair. "Like if she rented a car or booked a hotel room somewhere."

"That should be doable. You know... tracking her credit cards, debit cards, and bank account."

"But we also need to consider the possibility that Rachel never intended to leave," I said, taking another sip of my wine. "What if someone else bought the tickets in her name?"

Matt leaned forward. A frown grew between his eyes. "What do you mean?"

I shrugged. "Maybe someone did this to make it look like she was leaving—to fool us into thinking she left."

Matt's eyes widened. "That's a possibility too. But who would do that and why?"

I shrugged, my fingers fiddling with the stem of my wine

glass. I could feel the wine now and knew this would have to be my last glass of the night if I wanted to be able to work the next day.

"The husband would be my first choice," I said, "but that's just a guess. We need to dig deeper into her relationships before we can say anything real. I think we should also try to track down anyone else who might know something: friends, family, coworkers... even neighbors. Maybe someone knows something that could help us. We should also go back to Rachel's house tomorrow to see if we've missed anything. And I definitely want to talk to the sister and the mother."

Matt finished his beer and stood up. "Sounds like we have a busy day tomorrow. Guess we won't get anything done around the house again." He said the last part with a deep exhale. I knew exactly how he felt. But this was more important.

"It can wait," I said. "It's not going anywhere."

"I know. It's just...."

"Annoying, I know. To be living in this mess."

"And I really want to finish Elijah's room so he can move out of the nursery where he's sleeping with Angel."

"I know. It can't be fun being a pre-teen sleeping with a toddler. It's not sustainable—that's for sure, even though he has been such a great sport about it. I haven't heard him complain at all. That's really something. If it had been one of my teenagers, they wouldn't have been able to stop whining about it, driving me nuts."

"Yeah, he's a good boy," Matt said proudly.

He smiled. I was so happy having him on this case and by my side again. I really loved him. I couldn't believe it had taken me so many years to finally admit it to myself. He was my soulmate—my one and only.

"It's getting late," he said and yawned. "Let's get some rest and tackle this again tomorrow."

I nodded and followed him up the stairs to our bedroom. As we got ready for bed, I couldn't help but wonder what other surprises this case held. Would we ever discover what happened to Rachel, or would it remain a mystery forever? I knew it would haunt me for years to come if I couldn't figure it out. But I simply had to—for her children's sake. For Thomas.

Sleep eventually claimed me, but before it did, my mind still raced with possibilities and questions.

Chapter 6

Matt and I got out of the car, squinting into the glowing orange sky. A warm breeze rustled through the trees, carrying the faint smell of blooming gardenia. As we approached the house, an image came into view—two figures standing on the porch, waiting for us.

Kyla Johnson stepped forward, her hands shaking as she held up a picture of her missing sister. Her voice quivered as she said, "Please, you need to understand why this is so important to us."

Tears formed in her eyes.

The mother, Madeleine Johnson, then approached us and said, "My daughter has three children, two of them just toddlers. Their father is dangerous; he could... he could have...." She stopped mid-sentence, unable to finish the thought.

I felt my heart heavy with dread as Matt and I exchanged glances and went inside the house. As we entered, the musty scent of old furniture and decaying wood filled my nostrils. Madeleine Johnson led us to the living room, where we sat on a worn-out couch. The room was dimly lit, the shutters closed to keep out the sun and heat, and the only light source came from a lamp on a side table. On the wall hung a fedora hat behind glass. I looked at it, and Madeleine saw me.

"It's an original," she said with pride. "Michael Jackson autographed it inside. I never take it out."

"I take it you're a fan," I said, trying to ease the mood slightly and make them comfortable.

"Yes."

Matt cleared his throat before he began to speak. "I assume that you know we're here because we need to gather as much information as possible about the disappearance of your daughter, Rachel. I know you've been over this before, but we need to hear it again. When was the last time you saw her? When did you realize she was missing?"

The mother's eyes filled with tears as she spoke. "It was a week ago. We had dinner. I was supposed to babysit on the night she disappeared, but she hadn't told me what time. She and John were going out on a date—trying to mend their broken relationship. She never told me why they were struggling, but now that I hear this... that he was cheating, it all makes more sense. He was never good for her. I know he did something; I just know it in my heart."

Kyla placed a hand on her mother's arm to calm her.

"Sorry, yes. You were asking about when I realized she was missing. Well, when she didn't answer my calls or texts, I knew something was wrong. I called Kyla, and she hadn't heard from her either. Rachel always texts us during the day. We're very close that way. We always keep an eye out for one another, as families do."

Kyla chimed in, "She has three children, and she'd never leave them like that. I know my sister. Something's happened to her; I know it."

Matt nodded sympathetically and pulled out a notepad and pen. "Can you give us any information about her whereabouts before she went missing? Did she mention any plans or have any enemies?"

The mother shook her head, her eyes red from crying. "She didn't have any enemies that we know of. She worked long hours at the hospital. She was always tired, but she loved her kids more than anything. She wouldn't just disappear like this."

"She bought plane tickets for the day she disappeared," I said. "Do you know anything about her planning a trip?"

They glanced at one another, then shook their heads almost simultaneously. They were definitely mother and daughter, no doubt about that, as they looked so alike it was almost uncanny. Rachel looked very different from them, and I knew how that felt. My older sister, Sydney, looked just like my mom, tall, blonde, and gorgeous, whereas I took after my dad, short, stubby, and red-haired. But what can you do? You don't get to choose whose genes you get. I wondered where the dad was, but then I remembered reading in the file that he had never been in the picture.

"No, she would most definitely have mentioned that to us," Kyla said. "She wouldn't go on a trip without telling us, that's for sure."

"And you're certain she didn't just forget to tell you?" I asked.

Her mother shook her head violently. "No! Rachel told her sister and me everything. If she were going out of town, we would have been the first to know, right Kyla?"

Kyla nodded. "Yes. It's true."

I leaned forward, my eyes scanning the room for any clues. "Did she have any recent changes in behavior? Anything out of the ordinary?"

Kyla hesitated before answering. "Well, she did mention that John had cheated on her. More than once."

"What? It was more than once?" the mother said, appalled. She snorted angrily. "I knew he was no good for her. Do you think he had something to do with her disappearance?"

Matt scribbled something down in his notebook. "It's possible, but we can't jump to conclusions just yet. We'll need to look into John's whereabouts during the time Rachel went missing."

As we continued our conversation with the family, my mind raced with possibilities. Was John capable of harming his own wife?

"What about Kyla and Rachel's father?" I asked. "Could he have shown up suddenly? Did she have any contact with him?"

Her mother shook her head again. "No. He left when they were so young. She never knew him."

"Could she have tried to find him?" I asked. "Or maybe he tried to find her? Could he have contacted her?"

The mother scoffed. "I don't think so. It's impossible."

"Could we get his information just to check that angle?" I asked. "Also, if you know of any previous boyfriends or relationships she was in. We need to look into that as well."

The mother exhaled, annoyed. "You need to focus your energy on John. That's what you need to do."

"We will do that, too," Matt said.

"I fear that he might harm the children," the mother said after clearing her throat. "You can't let him get away with this. Please, bring my daughter back home."

Matt and I exchanged a look, both of us knowing that time was of the essence. We promised the family that we would do everything in our power to find Rachel and bring her home safely.

As we left the house, the warm breeze had turned into a strong wind as the afternoon thunderstorms approached. The gardenia scent was gone, replaced by the smell of rain as dark clouds gathered above us. I shivered, feeling a sense of foreboding wash over me.

"Boy, they were busy blaming it on the husband," I said, breaking the silence.

"I guess, but I think they're right. We need to look deeper into

John Baker," Matt said, holding the car door for me. "He didn't give me a good feeling when we met with him."

I nodded, feeling a knot form in my stomach. As we got into the car, I couldn't shake the fear that we were running out of time. And most importantly, I was also very worried about the children. If John Baker had hurt their mother, were they safe with him?

"I know what you mean, but I just don't like it when people try to tell me how to do my job, you know?"

Chapter 7

THEN:

On the surface, everything looked great. The parade of the girls glided down the street as it did every Saturday morning when their mother took them to the farmer's market—not so much to buy anything... usually just some honey and maybe a couple of apples. No, this was done to show them off, to show the world how fortunate and perfect they were. Each of the girls wore a soft blue dress of the finest quality. Emma, the oldest among them, had her light brown hair woven in an intricate braided bun that rested atop her head. Her feet moved with smooth deliberateness, perfectly in sync with her sisters' as they followed their mother at the head of the line.

Like small ducks in a row.

At the market or on their way there, they'd always stop to talk to neighbors from the street. The girls were expected to remain still, not utter a word unless spoken to, and keep it brief if asked a question.

A simple yes or no would do, of course, followed by a sir or ma'am for politeness.

Emma's heart raced as people praised the family for their perfect appearance. She could feel her mother's gaze upon her and saw slight disapproval in her eyes. She tried to walk even more erectly, holding her chin just a bit higher in hopes of not causing offense or provoking her mother's wrath. Each movement was careful and precise, and she was sure to stay in step with her siblings as if one false move could trigger unseen consequences.

The older girls were dressed in the same style, their dresses swaying ever so lightly with each step they took. Their mother, walking at the head of the line, smiled politely as people they passed praised her children.

"Oh, how pretty they all look!" one woman remarked.

Emma glanced up at her mother's face from time to time—nervously searching for any disapproving looks or signs of anger—and tried to keep her steps in perfect rhythm with those ahead. Every swish of a dress hem seemed to reverberate.

"Such a beautiful family," someone else said, no one addressing the fact that the girls' eyes all had a terrified look or that Emma's hands were shaking in fear.

The girls smiled and nodded as they had been taught, yet despite their appearance, an invisible current of fear traveled along the line, binding them together in a moment of reverie. Even the simplest of movements or actions could trigger the dreaded wrath of their mother, erasing any sense of security they had.

Emma's heart raced as she glanced up at her mother, who gave her a slightly disapproving look. She quickly adjusted her posture, walking with her chin just a bit higher, and tried to keep her steps in perfect unison with her siblings. She didn't want to be the one to make a mistake and incur the wrath of her mother.

As they walked, Emma couldn't help but glance around at the other children her age, laughing and playing without a care in the world. She longed to join in, to be free from the constant pressure of perfection. But she knew that was impossible. Her mother wouldn't allow it.

Suddenly, a gust of wind blew through the market, sending papers and fruit peels flying. Emma's dress fluttered around her legs, and startled at this, fighting to prevent it from happening, she stumbled, losing her place in line. She put her hands in front of her chest as she landed on the ground. Her heart racing, she looked up at her mother, waiting for the inevitable punishment.

But to her surprise, her mother simply reached out a hand, pulling her back into place.

"Be more careful, Emma," she said softly, a small smile on her lips, throwing a cautious glance around at the people looking at them. It wasn't much, but to Emma, it was a gift, a rare moment of kindness that she knew could be taken away at any moment.

And so, it was.

As soon as they made it back home and the door was closed behind them, all hell broke loose. It came out of the blue and startled Emma. Her mother approached her, moving fast, her eyes turning dangerously dark. She reached over and pinched her arm hard.

Emma winced in pain as her mother put her face close to hers.

"How could you embarrass me like that? How could you do that to me?"

"I'm... sorry...," she apologized, hoping her mother would let her go, but instead, her mother grabbed her hair and pulled her head back.

"Sorry doesn't cut it, Emma," she yelled. "You embarrassed me in front of everyone. God, you're worthless, child. You can't even walk without tripping, pah. I can't believe you're my daughter... doing that. No daughter of mine can't walk without stumbling; that's for sure."

Emma felt tears prick at the corners of her eyes, but she refused to let them fall. She knew that showing any sign of weakness would only make things worse. Experience had taught her that.

"I'll do better," she said quietly, hoping to placate her mother. But it was no use. Her mother continued to berate her, her words cutting like a thousand knives.

"You're darn right you will. How will I ever show my face again, huh? They're gonna think something is wrong with me for having a child like you, stumbling over her own darn feet. What's wrong with you?" Then she reached out and pinched her again, hard.

Emma winced in pain as tears streamed down her face. She knew better than to fight back or say anything other than "Yes, Mother" in a quiet voice.

Her mother finally released her and walked away, leaving her standing there alone and afraid. She felt her torso begin to shake, but she wouldn't let it. She took a deep breath, then simply wiped away her tears and began to straighten her dress, determined to keep up appearances. She had stumbled today and failed her mother, but it was never going to happen again. From now on, she was going to be perfect.

Part II

THURSDAY

Chapter 8

John Baker sat in his living room, tapping his fingers against the armrest of his chair. When the doorbell rang, John braced himself as he walked to open it. He opened it to find Mrs. Johnson's face on the other side, twisted into a mask of rage. He wasn't surprised to see her. He had expected her to show up.

"Where is my daughter?" she demanded, her voice tight with anger. "Where is my daughter?!"

John tried to maintain his composure. "Mrs. Johnson, Madeline, I'm sorry. I don't know where Rachel is."

But Mrs. Johnson was not listening. She pushed past him, barging into his house. "I demand to see the children. Where are the children!" she shouted.

John tried to stop her, but she was too strong. He followed her as she marched into the next room, calling out her grandchildren's names.

"Robert? Maria? Thomas? Your nanna is here."

But there was no response. She looked for toys in the living room, but they were all neatly in the box. No one had been playing with them.

Mrs. Johnson turned on him, her eyes blazing. "You've done something to Rachel. I just know you have. I always knew you were bad for her," she shouted. "And now the children are gone too? I demand to know... where are my grandchildren?"

John shook his head and said nothing.

Mrs. Johnson's face was red with anger. "I demand to see my grandchildren," she said again, her voice unsteady.

John took a deep breath and steeled himself.

"I'm sorry," he said. "But you can't."

Mrs. Johnson took a step forward, invading his personal space. "What do you mean I can't? They're my grandchildren, darn it!"

John backed away, feeling cornered. "I mean that they're not here, Madeline. They're not in the house."

Mrs. Johnson's eyes narrowed. "Then where are they?" she said, her voice low and dangerous.

John hesitated, unsure of what to say. He didn't want to tell her where he had taken them out of fear that they might be taken from him in the midst of all this while searching for his wife. But Mrs. Johnson was not going to let this go. She was like a pitbull; once she had her teeth in something, she wouldn't let go.

"They're safe," he said finally. "That's all you need to know. I've taken them somewhere safe."

Mrs. Johnson's face softened almost imperceptibly. "Safe from what?" she said, her voice quieter now.

John took another deep breath. "Safe from you," he said, his voice barely above a whisper.

Mrs. Johnson recoiled as if struck.

"What on earth are you talking about?" she said, her voice trembling.

Mrs. Johnson's eyes glinted with tears, but they were tears of rage. "How dare you judge me!" she shouted. "You don't know anything about me."

John's voice was steady.

"I know enough," he said. "Enough to know you are not fit to be around your grandchildren."

Mrs. Johnson took a step forward, her fists clenched. "You have no right to keep my grandchildren from me," she said, her voice boiling with anger.

John stood his ground. "I have every right. I am their legal guardian and will do whatever it takes to protect them."

Mrs. Johnson's face was still twisted with anger, but there was something else there, too—fear, maybe. Or perhaps it was just shock. He couldn't tell.

"You can't do this," she said, her voice trembling. "You can't take my grandchildren away from me."

"I already have," John said.

Mrs. Johnson's breath caught in her throat. "What do you mean?" she said, her voice barely audible.

John took a step forward. "I mean that I don't want them around you and your toxic environment," he said. "I have had enough."

Mrs. Johnson's face went white as a sheet. "You don't know what you're talking about."

John took another step forward. "I know enough," he said, his voice low and threatening. "You're not fit to be around children. Now, please, leave my house."

Mrs. Johnson backed away, her eyes wide with fear. She walked to the door and went out on the porch.

"Please," she said, her voice barely audible as she turned to face him in the doorway. "Please, don't do this."

But John was unmoved. "It's too late," he said, his voice hard. "It's already done. You won't see the children again."

Mrs. Johnson hid her face in her hands, tears streaming down her cheeks. "Please," she sobbed.

But John was resolute. "It's too late," he repeated. "You made your bed; now, you have to lie in it."

Mrs. Johnson buried her face in her hands, sobbing uncontrollably. John watched her for a moment, then turned and walked away, slamming the door shut behind him.

Mrs. Johnson saw this, then ran to it, hammering her fists onto it, yelling: "If you have hurt the children, I'll make sure you pay for it. Do you hear me? You will not get away with this. You will not!"

But John didn't hear her. He had locked the door, leaving her alone on the porch with her fit of rage.

Chapter 9

Matt and I sat in the quiet police station, the only sound coming from the occasional tapping of keys or slurping of coffee. We were both poring over the mound of documents and reports that we had piled up on the desk. Every lead we followed seemed to be a dead end, and as I sat at my desk at the police station, I couldn't help but feel a nagging sense of frustration. We just couldn't seem to catch a break. We had interviewed family, friends, and co-workers at the hospital; we had talked to witnesses driving by on the road seeing the abandoned car, but none of them had seen her actually stop and get out. We had looked into John's background, but nothing about him seemed to stick out as out of the ordinary—a couple of speeding tickets when he was younger and a bar fight. I couldn't help thinking we were looking in the wrong direction. Every time I thought of Rachel, I kept thinking about her father. Her mom hadn't seemed to want to talk about him much, which intrigued me. Why wasn't he in the picture? Why had he left the children when they were younger? No one seemed to want to answer that question. I needed to know if he had somehow been in contact with Rachel.

But then, something caught my eye as I sipped my freshly brewed coffee.

Matt was sitting at his desk, scrolling through his computer, a look of intense focus etched on his face. I sauntered over to him, peering over his shoulder to see what he was working on.

"Find something interesting?" I asked, taking another sip of my coffee.

Matt looked up, his eyes alight with excitement. "I found Rachel's father," he said, a hint of triumph in his voice.

My heart leaped at his words. We'd been struggling to find any leads, and if her father had anything to do with it, we might have finally caught a break.

"Where is he?" I asked, my voice barely above a whisper.

Matt turned his computer screen toward me, revealing a picture of a middle-aged man with an unkempt beard and piercing blue eyes.

"His name is David Parker," he said. "He's been living in Jacksonville for some years, but look where he is now."

"Prison."

I gasped, my heart beating faster with anticipation. "For what? What did he do?"

Matt leaned in closer to the computer screen, pointing at a list of charges. "Looks like first-degree murder."

I frowned, trying to connect the dots.

"Murder?"

I breathed the word out, feeling a sense of dread settle in my stomach. If Rachel's father was in prison, then what did that say about her? Was she in danger? Was he involved in her disappearance?

"Yes, murder... one of his own children, Rachel's older sister. And guess what? I just saw on the phone records that Rachel phoned a number in Jacksonville several times before she disappeared. Let me just check... Yup, it's the number to the prison he's in. She was in contact with him. How about that?"

"We need to talk to him," I said, my mind already racing with questions. "When can we go see him?"

Matt nodded, reaching for his phone. "I'll call the prison and see if we can schedule a visit." He paused, his eyes flicking back up to mine. "But we need to be careful. If he's involved in this, we don't want to give him any idea that we suspect him."

I nodded, knowing that he was right. If Rachel's father was involved, we didn't want to tip him off before we had all the evidence we needed. But at the same time, I couldn't shake the feeling that we were finally on the right track. My mind raced, trying to process the information. Could it be a coincidence, or was something more sinister at play? There was only one way to find out.

"We can see him today," Matt said, hanging up. I looked at my watch.

"We should get going. It's a two-and-a-half-hour drive to get there, so it will be late before we're back."

Matt made a face. "Can your mom pick up Angel and stay with the kids when they come home from school, do you think?"

"I'll ask."

Chapter 10

Kyla sat in the plush chair in the lawyer's office, her hands tightly clasped in her lap. Her mother sat beside her with her face etched with worry lines. They looked at the man in front of them as he sat down and pulled out a notepad.

"So, Mrs. Johnson, Miss Johnson," he said, looking at each of them. "I understand you're worried about your sister?"

Kyla nodded, her stomach clenching with anxiety. "Yes, we haven't heard from her in days. She's never gone this long without contacting us. We filed a missing person's report, and the police are working on finding her."

The lawyer scribbled something down on his notepad before looking up at them. "Do you have any reason to believe she's in danger?"

Kyla's mother nodded her head. "Yes, most definitely. She's been going through a tough time lately. Her marriage is falling apart, and she's been struggling with depression."

The lawyer nodded in understanding. "Before we do anything, I should tell you that it's possible that she just needs some time alone. People often disappear for a while when they're going through a difficult time."

Kyla's heart sank at the thought of her sister suffering alone. No, it wasn't just her running away. It couldn't possibly be.

"But what if she's hurt? What if she needs help?"

The lawyer sighed. "If you truly believe she's in danger, we can take legal action. But we need more evidence before we can do that."

Kyla's mother looked at her, eyes pleading. "We have to do something, Kyla. We can't just sit here and wait for the worst to happen."

Kyla nodded, determination settling in her heart. "I'll do whatever it takes to find her and make sure she's safe."

The lawyer shifted in his chair and cleared his throat. Kyla continued, desperation in her voice.

"Mr. White, we're really worried about my sister," she said, her voice shaking. "We don't know where she is. We think her husband might have something to do with it."

The lawyer, a tall, middle-aged man with thinning hair and a serious expression, leaned forward in his chair. "I'm sorry to hear that, Kyla. Can you tell me more details?"

Kyla took a deep breath and began to recount the details of her sister's troubled marriage. The infidelity and how her sister had married a man who was charming at first but quickly revealed himself to be controlling and abusive.

The lawyer listened intently as Kyla spoke, making notes on his notepad. It felt good to finally be heard. She didn't feel like the police took her seriously when she tried to explain to them how she believed John was a danger to both Rachel and the children. This guy seemed to get it.

"I see," he said once Kyla had finished. "This is definitely a cause for concern. Has your sister reported any incidents of abuse to the police?"

Kyla was about to answer when her mother placed a hand on her arm to hold her back.

Kyla's mother shook her head. "No, she's been too afraid."

"She was afraid of him? Was he physically abusive?"

"No, it was more mentally. Constantly controlling her every move, checking up on her, telling her she couldn't see her own family or even talk to us on the phone."

"Yet, you said you spoke every day?" he said.

"Mostly texts. Sometimes on the phone, but always when he wasn't around," she said. "She had to hide that she was talking to us. He never liked her family much and thought we had too much say in her life—that we meddled in their affairs. I think he just tried to isolate her. And now... now, I'm certain he has hurt her somehow. She wouldn't just disappear out of the blue like that—not my daughter."

The lawyer nodded grimly. "I understand. Mental abuse is a serious issue, and we need to take this into consideration." Kyla and her mother exchanged a look before the mom continued:

"We want to have the children. To protect them—from him."

"We don't believe they're safe with him," Kyla echoed.

The lawyer nodded and wrote down some notes. "I understand your concerns, but I need to remind you that custody battles can be complicated. We'll need evidence to prove that your sister's husband is unfit to care for the children."

Kyla's mother sighed. "I know, but we have to try. We can't just sit here and do nothing."

The lawyer leaned back in his chair, steepling his fingers in thought. "I see. I understand how you feel. I truly do. Well, it won't be easy, but we can certainly try. First, we'll need to gather as much evidence as possible against him: any proof of abuse, witnesses, anything that can help us make a case against him."

"We will get that for you, Mr. White," Kyla's mother said. "Trust me. We will get it if it's the last thing we do."

Chapter 11

The guard led us through a series of metal detectors and checkpoints. It had been a long drive up to Jacksonville, and I was feeling exhausted. I had eaten an entire bag of M&M's on the way and drank a lot of coffee, but it didn't seem to help much. And now, I felt guilty about eating all that junk. I had gotten better at staying away from that sort of food, and my weight had gone down, but now and then, I fell back in, and it bothered me.

We were shown inside and walked down the sterile, fluorescent-lit hallway of the prison, the sound of our footsteps echoing off the concrete walls. I felt a mix of nerves and excitement, unsure of what to expect. I really hoped we could get some answers here, but I also knew it could be a long shot.

His daughter was missing, yes, but chances were he wouldn't talk to us about it. Why would he?

The guard stopped, finally depositing us in a sterile visiting room. As we stepped into the room, I couldn't help but feel a sense of unease. We looked around anxiously, trying to spot Rachel's father.

And then we saw him. He sat at a table across the room, his face stony and unapproachable. We took a deep breath and walked over to him. I had read his case file. He was convicted of murdering his own daughter – Rachel's sister - when she was fourteen years old. That was the last time he had seen any of his children. I suddenly understood why the mother didn't want to talk about him. He claimed to be innocent during the whole trial, but the evidence against him had been too convincing. He smirked when he saw us, then tilted his head.

"Detectives, welcome to my humble abode. What can I do for you?"

I tried to push the gruesome details of his past out of my mind and focus on the task at hand. "We're here because we're investigating the disappearance of your daughter, Rachel. We were hoping you could answer a few questions for us," I said, trying to keep my tone neutral.

He raised an eyebrow. "Rachel? I haven't seen her in years—since she was a young child, if I remember well. We don't exactly keep in touch," he said, his tone dripping with sarcasm.

I exchanged a glance with Matt. We both knew he was lying. We knew he had been in contact with Rachel just days before she disappeared.

"Mr. Parker, we have reason to believe you spoke to Rachel before she went missing. Can you tell us about that?" I asked, cutting right to the chase.

He leaned back in his chair, a smug expression on his face. "Oh, I see. You think I had something to do with her disappearance. Well, I hate to disappoint you, but I haven't spoken to Rachel in years. And even if I had, why would I have any reason to harm my own daughter?" he scoffed.

I could feel my patience wearing thin. "We're not accusing you of anything, Mr. Parker. We just want to find Rachel and bring her home. If you have any information that could help us, we urge you to come forward," I said, my tone firm. "Did she come to see you? Did she plan to come here?"

He leaned forward, his eyes narrowing. "I don't know where Rachel is. And even if I did, do you think I would tell you? You're just trying to pin this on me because of what happened in the past. I'm already serving time for something I didn't do. I've been in here all this time; how on earth could I have hurt Rachel?" he muttered, his tone turning defensive.

Matt stepped in, his voice calm but assertive. "Mr. Parker, we're not trying to punish you for your past crimes. We're just trying to find your daughter. When she called, what did you two talk about?"

Mr. Parker looked at Matt with a seething gaze, "I already told you; I haven't spoken to Rachel in years. And even if I had, I wouldn't share our private conversations with you two. You're just trying to manipulate me into giving you information you can use against me," he growled, his fists clenched tightly.

I took a deep breath, trying to keep my cool. "We understand you might be hesitant to share information with us, Mr. Parker. But please understand that we're trying to help Rachel. She's been missing for days, and we're running out of time. Any information you can give us could be the difference between finding her safe and sound or not," I said, my tone gentle.

He glared at me for a moment, then leaned back in his chair, his face expressionless. "Fine. Rachel did call me a few days ago."

Mr. Parker's expression changed at the mention of their conversation. He looked down at the table, his hands fidgeting with the edge of the table. "She, uh, she called me because she was in trouble. She said she needed some money and a place to stay for a couple of days. I told her I couldn't help her," he said, his voice barely above a whisper.

"Why didn't you mention this before?" I asked, my voice stern.

He looked up at us, his eyes hardening. "Because I didn't want to be involved. As I said, I haven't seen Rachel in years. She's an adult now; she can take care of herself," he said, his voice cold.

Matt leaned forward, his eyes locked on Mr. Parker's. "But you sent her the money, didn't you?"

Mr. Parker's eyes darted away, unable to meet Matt's intense gaze. "I don't know what you're talking about," he muttered.

"Mr. Parker, we're not stupid. We know you sent her money," Matt said, his voice steady.

Mr. Parker's eyes widened in surprise. "How do you know that?" he asked, his voice betraying his fear.

"You just told us," Matt said simply.

"Fine. Yes, I sent her some money. But that's all I know. She didn't tell me where she was or what she was doing," he said, his voice defeated.

I leaned forward, my eyes locked on his. "Mr. Parker, if Rachel is in trouble, we need to know. We can protect her, but we need to find her first. Please, tell us everything you know," I pleaded.

He looked at me for a long moment, his eyes searching mine. And then he spoke. "That's all I know. I swear."

I could see by the defeated look on his face that he was telling the truth and let it go.

"So, you did send her the money?" Matt asked. "Why would you do that if you haven't seen her in years?"

Mr. Parker hesitated for a moment before speaking. "I wanted to help her, okay? She's still my daughter, no matter what happened in the past. I knew it took a lot of courage for her to contact me at all. She had to be in very serious trouble. I didn't want her to be out on the streets with nowhere to go," he said, his voice shaking slightly.

I could see the emotion on his face, and suddenly, I felt a pang of sympathy for him. Despite what he had done in the past, he was still a father who cared about his child.

"Did Rachel say anything else to you?" I asked gently.

He shook his head. "No, that was all. She just asked for the money and a place to stay. I told her I couldn't give her a place to stay, but I sent her the money anyway. That's all I know," he said.

Matt and I exchanged a look. We knew that Mr. Parker was holding something back, but there was nothing more we could do to get the information out of him. As we left the visitation room, I couldn't help but feel conflicted about Mr. Parker. On one hand, he had committed a heinous crime in the past and had shown little remorse for his actions. But on the other hand, he had helped Rachel when she needed it, despite their estranged relationship. It was a complicated situation, and I knew we still had a long way to go before we found Rachel and brought her home. As we walked to our car, I couldn't shake the feeling that we were missing something important, but I didn't know what it was. We got into the car and drove back to the station, our minds racing with the possibilities of what could have happened to Rachel. The big question was whether she was still alive.

Chapter 12

THEN:

Emma and her two younger sisters sat nervously in the photographer's studio. They had been waiting to have their family portraits taken for what felt like hours, and now, it was finally their turn. Standing next to the photographer, their mother was inspecting every detail of the set-up, her eyes scanning the room for flaws. Emma and her sisters sat in front of the photographer in their Sunday best. The studio was quiet except for the occasional click of the camera.

"Emma, sit up straight," their mother said, adjusting her daughter's posture. "And smile, but not too big. You don't want to show too many teeth. No one wants to see those big gums of yours."

Emma forced a smile, feeling self-conscious under her mother's critical eye. Her sisters fidgeted in their seats, trying to hold back their giggles.

Their mother continued to fuss over them, making tiny adjustments to their hair and clothing. "Now, Lily, tilt your head a bit to the left. And Lily, put your hand on your hip."

The photographer tried to capture the moment, but it was obvious that he could sense the tension in the room.

"Okay, everyone. Let's take a deep breath and relax," he said.

But their mother couldn't let go of her perfectionism. "No, no, we need to get this right. Emma, fix your hair. It's a mess."

Emma sighed, her curls bouncing as she tried to tame them.

The photographer cleared his throat and began placing them in position. "Okay, everyone, let's start with the basic family portrait. Everyone, look at the camera and smile!"

Emma forced a smile, but her mom quickly interrupted. "No, that's not right. Smile with your teeth, Emma. And Lily, close your mouth a little bit. You look like a fish."

The photographer snapped a quick shot before their mom continued. Emma and her sisters obliged, but their smiles quickly faded as their mother spoke.

"Emma! How many times must I say this? Sit up straighter. And Lily, close your mouth a bit more. And Emma, don't scrunch up your nose like that. We need these pictures to turn out perfectly," their mother said, her voice sharp.

The girls tried to follow their mother's directions, but it seemed like no matter what they did, it wasn't good enough. The photographer snapped picture after picture, but their mother kept requesting retakes, nitpicking every detail.

Emma felt a knot forming in her stomach as the photographer began to look increasingly uncomfortable. She wished her mother could just let go and allow them to be themselves, to enjoy the moment without the constant pressure to be perfect. But she knew that was unlikely to happen.

Just when Emma thought the photoshoot couldn't get any worse, their mother had a new bright idea.

"Okay, let's do a silly one now! Everyone, make a funny face!"

Emma's heart sank as she saw the look of dread on her

younger sisters' faces. They knew from experience that their mother's idea of "silly" was not the same as theirs.

Emma reluctantly contorted her face into a goofy expression, but her sisters were less successful. Lily looked more like she was in pain, and the youngest struggled to keep a straight face.

Their mother was not amused. "Come on, girls! This is supposed to be fun. Let loose a little bit!" But her words only seemed to make things worse. Their forced laughter sounded stiff and awkward, and Emma was starting to feel embarrassed.

Finally, after what felt like hours, the photoshoot was over. The photographer packed up his equipment, and Emma and her sisters breathed a collective sigh of relief.

As they were leaving the studio, their mother turned to them with a smile on her face. "That was fun, wasn't it?" she asked, oblivious to the tension that had filled the room. "We'll have to come back again next year."

Emma and her sisters kept their thoughts to themselves, knowing there was no point in arguing with their mother. As they walked out into the sunlight, Emma couldn't help but feel a sense of relief that the ordeal was over.

As they got into the car, she sat down in the passenger seat with a deep sigh and put her seatbelt on while her mother helped the younger ones get into their seats. Then the door opened, and her mother sat in the driver's seat. She looked at Emma, a smile growing on her face. Then she lifted her fist, clenched it, and slammed it into Emma's temple.

Emma's head jerked to the side. Her vision blurred for a moment, and she could taste blood in her mouth. Shocked and confused, Emma looked at her mother, who was staring straight ahead, her grip on the steering wheel so tight that her knuckles were white.

Her mother's eyes flickered to her, and Emma could see a wild look in them, a look that scared her.

"You ruined those pictures, Emma—you and your sisters. You can't even follow simple instructions," her mother spat out. "You embarrassed me in there. You couldn't even make a decent silly face. How dare you embarrass me like that in front of the photographer! You were slouching, your hair was a mess, and your smile was crooked. I can't believe you would ruin our family portraits like that."

Emma could feel the anger boiling inside her, but she knew better than to say anything else. Her mother was not in a rational state of mind, and she didn't want to provoke her any further.

Silent tears streamed down Emma's face as her mother started the car and drove them home. The ride felt like an eternity, the tension in the air so thick that it felt like she would explode. But she didn't dare. The car ride was silent except for the sound of their mother's ragged breaths. Emma's sisters, sitting in the back seat, were too scared to say anything either.

When they finally got home, Emma opened the door and stepped out of the car with her mother close behind. As she walked toward the house, she could feel her mother's eyes drilling holes into the back of her head. She felt so embarrassed about herself and how she had behaved. Why couldn't she be better? Was it really that hard?

Chapter 13

I knew the moment I stepped through the door that something was wrong. The smell of bleach and cleaning solution hit me like a ton of bricks, and I had to fight off a wave of guilt that threatened to pierce my chest. Even before I stepped into the kitchen, I could hear somebody scrubbing something with a furious intensity.

My mom was on her hands and knees, a sponge in one hand and a rag in the other, scrubbing the already spotless kitchen floor with a vigor that betrayed her anxiety. For a moment, I felt like a small child again, standing at the entrance to the kitchen, unsure of how to proceed.

"Hey, Mom," I said, trying to sound casual as I kicked off my shoes.

My mom didn't even look up from her cleaning.

"Mom, it's clean enough now. Would you stop?"

She looked up, then snorted at me. "It's so dirty in this house. How can you let your children grow up in this mess?"

"Well, we are in the middle of renovations, Mom," I said. "So, it's only natural to have some dust, dirt, and mess."

"And what's going on with Elijah's room? Why doesn't he have a door? Why is he sleeping with the baby? Why doesn't the boy have his own room?"

"We're working on it," I said.

"You were gone all day, so it doesn't look like you're working on it," she said.

"Hey, we're on a case, okay? We've got jobs to do, too."

I walked to the wine fridge and pulled out a bottle. My mom made a noise behind me.

"What?" I asked. "I'm not allowed to have a glass of wine after a long day?"

She looked away. "I guess it's none of my business."

Matt grabbed a beer and then walked to the living room, getting away from us as fast as possible. I couldn't blame him.

I took a sip of the wine, relishing the taste and the way it soothed my nerves. My mom's presence always had a way of making me feel like a teenager again, and I hated it. I wanted to be able to live my own life without her constantly breathing down my neck.

"You know, Mom," I said, trying to keep my voice steady. "It's not easy being a detective. We see some pretty messed up things on a daily basis, and sometimes we need to unwind a little."

"I know that," she said, still scrubbing away at the floor. "But that doesn't mean you have to live in squalor."

I rolled my eyes. "It's not squalor, Mom. It's just a little messy. And we're in the process of renovating, remember?"

"I remember," she said, finally standing up and putting her cleaning supplies away. "I just worry about you. You're my baby, after all. I would never let you grow up in a mess like this. Never."

I sipped my wine, trying to push away the guilt lingering in my chest. I knew my mom meant well, but her constant need to clean and criticize only added to the weight on my shoulders. As I sat on the couch, I couldn't help but feel like a failure as a mother.

Matt sat down next to me, taking a swig of his beer before pulling me into a side hug. I leaned my head on his shoulder, taking comfort in his warmth and presence.

"It's okay, love," he whispered. "She's just worried about us."

"I know," I whispered back. "But I can't help but feel like I'm failing everyone."

"You're not failing anyone," Matt said firmly. "We're all doing our best, and that's all anyone can ask for."

I sighed, taking another sip of my wine. "I just wish she would understand that we have other things going on too. It's not just about cleaning and tidying up."

"I know, but she's just old-fashioned like that," Matt said, rubbing my arm soothingly. "She means well, but you don't have to listen to everything she says."

I nodded, taking another sip of wine and feeling the tension slowly leave my body. It was true that my mom meant well, but sometimes, her constant need for cleanliness and order could be suffocating. As I leaned back against the couch, I made a silent promise to myself to try and let go of the guilt and pressure I felt whenever I was around her. After all, I had my own family now, and it was up to me to create a warm and welcoming home, even if it wasn't always spotless.

I took another sip of my wine, leaned into Matt's embrace, and pushed my worries aside, focusing on the present moment and the love surrounding me. As I dozed off, I couldn't stop thinking about Rachel and how she was apparently in a rush to leave. She was getting money from a dad she didn't know and booking plane tickets. Why was that?

What was she running from?

What could make a mother run from her own family? And leave her children?

I could only think of one thing, one explanation strong enough to make me do that.

Danger.
She had to have felt like she was in danger somehow.

Chapter 14

John wiped the beads of sweat from his forehead with the back of his hand. He took a deep breath as he surveyed the living room. The furniture was gleaming, the carpets had been vacuumed, and every surface was dust-free. But there was still so much more to do. He glanced at the clock on the wall and saw it was already midday. He had been cleaning for hours, but he had committed to finishing the entire house today. The sun was blazing outside, and it was only getting hotter with each passing minute. Despite the fans blowing in every room and the AC on, there was no escaping the heat. He wiped the sweat from his forehead again and continued.

He scrubbed the tiles in the kitchen, dusted off the shelves, and wiped down every surface. He cleaned the countertops, washed the dishes, and mopped the floors.

As he moved on to the bedrooms, he could feel the sweat pouring down his back. But he didn't stop. He opened the windows to let in some fresh air, grabbed a mop and bucket of water, and headed to the bathroom, scrubbing it all down thoroughly.

He picked up the trash can and made his way to the kitchen. The smell of garbage hit him as he opened the lid, and he wrinkled his nose in disgust.

By the time he got to take out the trash, he was exhausted. But he knew it had to be done. He gathered all the garbage bags and dragged them outside to the dumpster. The strong scent of the trash mixed with the hot air made him want to gag, but he held his breath as he threw the bags into the bin.

As he made his way back inside, he paused for a moment, feeling the breeze on his skin. He looked up at the clear blue sky and closed his eyes, enjoying the brief moment of relief.

But when he opened them again, he saw something that made him freeze. A car was parked across the street, and inside sat a woman holding a pair of binoculars.

It was Rachel's mom.

What the heck?

John stared at her, bewildered, anger rising inside him, his nostrils flaring. He watched her for a few more moments, hoping she would leave, but she didn't budge.

John sighed heavily. He walked over to her car and tapped on the window. Rachel's mom rolled down the window.

"Can I help you?" John asked, trying to keep his tone polite.

"I was just checking up on you," Rachel's mom said, smiling sweetly.

John's eyebrows furrowed. "I'm not sure I understand."

Rachel's mom laughed sarcastically. "Oh, don't play dumb. You know exactly why I'm here."

John's heart started to race. He had a feeling he knew where this was going. "You need to leave. Now."

Rachel's mom snickered. "Or what? You'll call the cops?"

John's fists clenched. He could feel anger bubbling inside him. "If I have to, I will."

"Or maybe you'll kill me? Like you killed my daughter?"

He snorted in anger, then slammed his hand on the side of the car. "You bitch. If I ever see you here again...."

Rachel's mom shrugged. "Suit yourself." She rolled up the window and drove off, leaving John to stand in the scorching heat, feeling rattled and violated. John stood there, staring at her retreating car until it was out of sight, making sure she didn't come back. Then, he went back inside and realized he had missed a spot of blood on the wall in the living room. With a sigh, he grabbed a sponge and scrubbed it off.

Chapter 15

I sat in a dimly lit room at the police station, staring at the computer screen in front of me. The screen displayed the call logs from Rachel's phone, and I couldn't help but feel a knot forming in my stomach as I scrolled through the records.

There were several calls made in the middle of the night, each lasting only a few seconds. The number registered as "no caller ID," but the phone company had still managed to log the number.

I leaned closer to the screen, squinting as I tried to make out the digits.

I jotted down the numbers on a notepad, determined to find out who was responsible for those mysterious calls. It was clear that they were linked to Rachel's disappearance, and I wasn't going to stop until I found out the truth.

As I stood up from the desk, I felt a sense of urgency rise in me. I called the number.

The line rang for a few seconds before a woman picked up the phone. Her voice was low and husky, the kind that made my hair stand on end.

"Hello?" she said, her tone questioning.

"Who is this?" I asked, trying to keep my voice steady.

"Who's asking?" she countered.

I took a deep breath, trying to keep my frustration in check.

"My name is Eva Rae Thomas; I'm a detective at Cocoa Beach Police. I'm calling about Rachel Baker." I said, hoping that she would give me something, anything.

There was a pause on the other end of the line, and I could hear her breathing. Finally, she spoke again.

"I don't know what you're talking about," she said, her voice just as low as before.

I felt my anger growing, but I forced myself to stay calm.

"Listen, we're trying to find Rachel Baker, who has been reported missing, and we can see that your number has called her phone on several occasions in the middle of the night and then hung up."

The woman on the other end of the line was silent for a few moments before she spoke again. "I have no idea who Rachel Baker is," she said, her voice cold and devoid of emotion. "And I have certainly never called her phone."

I frowned, not quite sure what to make of her response. "Then why does your number show up on her call log?" I asked, trying to keep the frustration out of my voice.

"I don't know," the woman said, and I could practically hear the shrug in her voice. "Maybe someone is using my number to make those calls. It wouldn't be the first time someone stole my identity."

I didn't quite buy her explanation, but I didn't have any solid evidence to refute it either. "Can you at least give me your name?" I asked, hoping to get some kind of lead.

"Sorry, Detective," the woman said, a hint of amusement creeping into her voice. "I don't give my name to strangers over the phone. Goodbye." And with that, she hung up.

I stared at the phone in disbelief, feeling frustrated and

defeated. It was obvious that the woman on the other end of the line was lying, but I couldn't prove it.

I took a deep breath and tried to calm myself. I needed a new approach.

I looked down at the notepad in my hand—at the digits. Maybe there was a way to trace the number and find out who was really behind those calls.

I picked up the phone again, dialing the number for the tech department at the police station.

"Hey, it's Eva Rae Thomas," I said when someone picked up. "I need your help tracing a number."

And so, I spent the next few hours working with the tech department, trying to trace the mysterious number. It was a long shot, but I had nothing to lose.

They said they'd get back to me, and I hung up and returned to my computer when I heard turmoil coming from downstairs. A loud voice was yelling. I ran down the stairs and saw the woman manning our front desk, trying to calm a woman down. A police officer was telling her to back off.

I recognized the woman right away and exhaled. It was Rachel's mom.

"I demand to talk to the detectives, now!" she yelled.

"You have to wait," the officer said, "until they have time."

"It's okay," I said. They all three turned to look at me. "I'll talk to her. I'll take care of it."

Chapter 16

I could see the pain in Rachel's mother's eyes as we sat in the small room in the back of the police station downstairs. She looked like she had been crying for hours. I could feel my heart racing as I asked her what was going on.

"Mrs. Johnson, what's going on? Why did you come to talk to us?" I asked, my voice low and steady.

"I have proof that John killed my daughter," she said, her voice trembling. "He was cleaning his house, taking out big bags of trash."

I felt a chill run down my spine. "Really? Proof?" I asked, trying to keep my voice calm.

"Yes," she said.

"What kind of proof?"

She gave me a look of confusion. "I just told you. He cleaned his house."

I leaned toward Mrs. Johnson, staring directly into her eyes. "I understand that you're upset, but cleaning his house doesn't equate to proof of murder," I said, trying to keep my tone gentle.

"But the man has never cleaned anything in his life. Rachel did the cleaning; he never lifted a finger. Why is he suddenly doing that? Don't you find it suspicious?"

I couldn't deny the logic in Mrs. Johnson's words, but I needed more than just a cleaning spree to accuse John of murder. "Mrs. Johnson, we will investigate this thoroughly, but we need more evidence to prove that John committed a crime," I said, trying again to reassure her.

She let out a sigh, "I just want justice for my daughter, Detective. Please, find out the truth."

I nodded, "We will do our best, Mrs. Johnson. But for now, I need you to go home and try to get some rest. We will contact you as soon as we have any updates."

"Is that it?"

I could feel my stomach drop as I realized Mrs. Johnson's evidence was weak. I had hoped there was more to it than that. I really had wanted there to be. I needed a break in this case. But I also needed more than just a suspicion to bring someone to justice. I took a deep breath and leaned forward in my seat, trying to convey a sense of understanding and support to Rachel's mother.

"I know this is a difficult time for you, Mrs. Johnson. But we need to be absolutely sure before making any arrests or even treating someone as a suspect. Do you have any other evidence that might help us?" I asked, my voice carefully measured.

She looked down at her hands, and for a moment, I thought she might break down. But then she looked back up at me with fierce determination in her eyes.

"I don't have any physical evidence, but I know John did it," she said, her voice rising with conviction.

I nodded slowly, taking in her words. I knew that sometimes gut instincts could be powerful evidence in their own right. But I also knew that I needed to tread carefully. If I made any mistakes or missteps, it could derail the entire investigation.

"Mrs. Johnson, we're still doing everything we can to find Rachel," I said, trying to offer her some reassurance. "But so far, we have no idea what happened to her. We need to have concrete evidence before we can make any arrests. Can you think of anything else that might help us?"

She shook her head, looking defeated. "No, I'm sorry. I just want justice for my daughter. I want to know what happened to her. I need closure."

"I understand that," I said, standing up from my seat. "We'll keep investigating and let you know if we find anything that can help."

I could feel the weight of her pain and grief, and it broke my heart.

"All right, Mrs. Johnson. We'll look into this further," I said, leaning forward in my chair. "In the meantime, I suggest you take care of yourself and your family."

She scoffed. "Is that really the best you can do?"

"For now, yes."

She snorted at me. "Can't you just arrest him? So he won't harm the children too? He's taken them away, you know. We don't know where they are. And he's been threatening toward me. He has threatened her before, too—to take her children away from her."

"I understand your worry, Mrs. Johnson, but you need to trust us to do our job."

She stood to her feet. "Well, I don't. And meanwhile, he is removing all the evidence, and he will get away with murdering my daughter."

I stared at her as she rushed toward the door. I was worried. I was very worried about Rachel and the children, but my hands were tied. I couldn't do anything as of right now. So far, Rachel could have just left. There were no signs of a crime being committed.

As I left the room, I couldn't shake the feeling that something was off. Mrs. Johnson's evidence was flimsy at best, and I wasn't convinced that John was the killer. But I also knew I had to keep an open mind and consider all possibilities. My mind was racing with different theories and possibilities. Was John really the killer? Or was Mrs. Johnson just desperate to find someone to blame? I couldn't shake off the feeling that something was off about John. She was definitely right about that. The way he had been acting since Rachel's disappearance was suspicious. I knew I had to dig deeper, but I also knew I had to be careful not to make any mistakes that could jeopardize the case. With a heavy heart, I left the station, determined to find the truth about Rachel's disappearance, no matter what it took.

That night, I couldn't stop thinking about the case. I reviewed the interviews I had conducted with John and his family, trying to find any inconsistencies or signs of guilt. But everything seemed to be in order, and I couldn't find anything concrete to tie John to Rachel's disappearance. But there was no alibi either for the time of her disappearance.

I decided to visit John's house early the next morning while Matt went into the station to be at the morning briefing. I was hoping to find something that would help me in the investigation. As I approached the house, I saw John outside, pacing frantically. He looked up as he saw me, and his face turned pale.

"What are you doing here?" he asked, his voice shaking.

"I need to ask you a few more questions, John," I said, trying to keep my tone calm. "Can we go inside and talk?"

John hesitated for a moment, then nodded. I followed him inside the house and into the living room—his very clean living room. As we sat down, I couldn't help but notice how tense he was. His hands were shaking, and he was fidgeting with his shirt sleeve. His eyes darted around the room, avoiding mine. I decided to start with some basic questions to see if he would slip up.

"John, can you tell me about the last time you saw Rachel?" I asked, leaning forward slightly.

He swallowed nervously. "I already told you everything, Detective," he said, still avoiding eye contact.

"I know, but sometimes people remember things they forgot to mention before," I said, trying to coax him into talking more. "Did she say anything about where she was going or who she was meeting?"

He shook his head. "No, she didn't. She was going to work. That's all I know. She dropped me off at my office, said goodbye, then drove off."

"Did anyone see you being dropped off? Any of your colleagues?"

"You know they didn't. You've already asked them about it," he said.

"Maybe someone else saw you get out of the car? An old friend or someone working at the restaurant next door?"

"The restaurant doesn't open until five o'clock, so no one was there. You know this."

"So, you decided to walk down to the beach. Was that because you and Rachel were fighting?" I asked. "Did you need some time to calm down?"

"No. We weren't fighting."

I could tell he was lying, but that was hardly enough. I decided to change tactics and see if I could get him to slip up in a different way.

"John, can you explain why you cleaned your house so thoroughly the other day?" I asked, watching his reaction carefully.

His eyes widened in surprise. "What do you mean?"

"I mean, why were you cleaning so much when you've never done it before?" I pressed.

He hesitated for a moment, and I could see the sweat starting to bead on his forehead. "I just wanted everything to be perfect," he said, his voice trembling. Then he shrugged. "I don't know. I guess I just felt like the house needed a good cleaning."

I didn't buy it. "John, you've never cleaned the house before. Why start now?"

He shifted uncomfortably in his seat. "I don't know. Maybe I just felt like I had to do something."

"Something like what?" I asked, leaning in closer. "Something like hiding evidence?"

He looked at me in shock. "What are you talking about? I didn't hide anything."

"Then why were you cleaning so much?" I asked again, my voice firm.

He hesitated, then looked down at his hands. "Fine. I guess I was just trying to distract myself from everything that was happening. Rachel's disappearance is really taking a toll on me."

"That's understandable."

I leaned back in my chair, studying him. His behavior was suspicious, but I still had nothing concrete to tie him to Rachel's disappearance. I decided to push a little harder to see if I could get him to crack.

"John, if you know anything about Rachel's disappearance, now is the time to tell me," I said, my voice firm.

He looked me in the eye, and for a moment, I thought he was ready to confess. But then he looked away, his hands shaking even more violently than before.

"I don't know anything; I swear," he said, his voice barely above a whisper.

"Then why are you so nervous, John?" I asked, pressing on. "Why won't you make eye contact with me?"

He shook his head. "I just... I don't know. This whole thing has me on edge. I keep thinking that she left me and won't come back. It's all my fault for not treating her right. I know she never forgave me for it, but still. What kind of a mother leaves her children? I'm still hoping and praying that she'll come home. If not for me, then for the children's sake. Also, I fear she might have killed herself. That's my biggest fear right now."

"Why would she do that?" I asked.

"She wasn't in a good place. She was drinking a lot and often. I had told her she needed to stop if she wanted to keep her children and me around. I might have been too harsh. She was an alcoholic."

I didn't believe him. Why was this suddenly coming to the surface now? Why hadn't he mentioned anything about this earlier? When I asked if she was suicidal? It made no sense. It seemed like he was just trying to lead me in other directions. I didn't like that one bit. But I also knew I couldn't force a confession out of him, at least not yet. I decided to end the interview for now, hoping that I could gather more evidence before confronting him again.

"All right, John. I'll be in touch if I need anything else," I said, standing up from my chair. "Thank you for your time."

As I stood up to leave, John looked up at me with a desperate expression.

"Please, Detective. You have to find her. Rachel means everything to me," he said, his voice breaking.

I nodded, feeling a pang of sympathy for him but still unsure about his sincerity. It felt forced.

"We'll do everything we can, John. We won't stop until we find her."

He nodded, his hands still shaking. As I left the living room, I paused by the wall close to the door. It had been scrubbed recently, I could tell, as the paint was faded in an area. It had gotten a serious scrubbing. I made a mental note of it, then left.

I drove to the station and couldn't shake the feeling that he was guilty. But of what? Had he killed his wife? Or was she still out there?

Part III

THREE DAYS LATER

Chapter 17

Lena Watson hated going to her storage unit. It was dark and dingy, and the smell of mildew clung to the air like a ghost that refused to move on. She had tried her best to keep the place organized, but the narrow aisles between the units and the thick layer of dust still made her feel uneasy whenever she ventured there. But today, she needed something from her unit, so she reluctantly made the trip. She parked in front of the door and then sighed deeply. She hadn't been there to see her things since her mother died. She didn't know what to do with her stuff, but she couldn't bear the thought of getting rid of it either. She took a deep breath, then pushed open the door to her unit.

As she stepped inside, Lena felt a familiar sense of dread wash over her. The space was smaller than she remembered, and everything seemed to be coated in a thick layer of dust. She coughed as she kicked up some of the debris, then made her way to the back corner where her mother's things were stored. The smell hit her hard. It was bad. She coughed and waved at the air, trying to clear the dust that threatened to choke her. Her eyes flicked around the space, taking in the familiar boxes and trinkets she had stored away.

Lena's eyes adjusted to the darkness, and she could see the outlines of boxes and furniture scattered around the unit. She started to rummage through the boxes, her hands shaking as she went through each item, memories flooding back to her. She found herself lost in the past until she felt something brush against her leg.

She jumped back, her heart racing, until she realized it was just a stray cat that had snuck into her unit. It was skinny and dirty with matted fur, but it still managed to purr as it rubbed against her legs. There were a ton of them living in the area. The old woman who lived in a van in the parking lot always fed them. The manager let her live there since she was crazy as a bat, they said. She had nowhere else to go and lived off what the church folks next door gave to her, and she gave most of it to the cats.

As Lena rummaged through her unit, she again noticed a foul smell. She tried to ignore it, but it lingered and made her feel like gagging. She walked outside, trying to follow the smell, then realized it was coming from the unit next to hers. It was so bad that she had to cover her nose with her shirt. And there was something liquid seeping out from underneath the unit's roll-up door. The smell from it made her eyes water and her nose burn. Lena tried to hold her breath as she approached the unit next to hers. She could feel her heart pounding as she stared at the brown door. The stench hit her like a brick wall, making her gag and choke. She covered her mouth and nose with her hand and tried to steady her breathing.

Lena had an overwhelming urge to investigate. She knew she shouldn't, but she couldn't help herself. Curiosity had always been her weakness. She walked over to the unit and peeked through the small opening at the bottom of the garage door, using her phone as a flashlight. She immediately regretted it. The smell was nearly unbearable. But that wasn't the worst of it. Lena's eyes locked onto a small hand sticking out from underneath a black tarp.

It was pale and lifeless.

Lena stumbled back, bile rising in her throat. She knew she had to call the police. She reached for her phone but stopped when she heard footsteps approaching. She turned her head with a loud gasp, looked behind her, and saw the old woman who fed the cats standing there. She was standing there on her skinny legs, staring at Lena, her eyes looking at her from inside a weathered face. They locked eyes briefly, and Lena saw a strange glint in the old woman's eyes. It terrified her to the core. Lena gasped and pulled back. She knew the woman was crazy. Would she harm her? Lena feared for a second she would, but it didn't happen. Instead, the old woman turned and walked away, her feet shuffling along the concrete floor.

Lena's heart raced as she dialed 9-1-1 and put the phone to her ear.

Chapter 18

As I stood at the stove, the smell of sizzling bacon filling the air, I couldn't help but feel a sense of pride in my family. Two of my children, Alex and Christine, came bouncing down the stairs, their energy filling the room—well, Alex's at least. Christine had that teenage air about her that signaled that no one should try to talk to her until later in the day. My oldest, Olivia, was a senior and didn't have to get to school until later, so she was still sleeping. She had previously told me that she believed she was non-binary, but now she was back to being a she and a her again and had announced that she was a lesbian instead. I told her I didn't care if she was a purple dinosaur as long as she was happy.

Alex and Christine sat at the kitchen counter, Alex drumming his fingers on the granite surface and eagerly surveying the scene. Christine glanced up briefly from her phone before returning to it with a single-minded focus. Moments later, Matt's son Elijah stumbled down the stairs, rubbing sleep from his eyes and immediately reaching for his phone. Alex was soon hunched over a plate of eggs and bacon with a fork in hand. His eyes were wide with anticipation while Christine swiped across her phone's screen with one hand.

I served Christine a pancake, and she wrinkled her nose.

"Do you want bacon and eggs instead?" I asked. "You usually prefer pancakes."

She scoffed. "Don't you have any fruit?"

I lifted my eyebrows. "For once, I make you pancakes, and now you don't want them? I'm trying to be a good mom here."

She groaned. "A good mom would serve me something healthy."

Oh, dear, here we go.

"Grandma always serves us vegan pancakes and gluten-free stuff."

"Oh, does she, now?" I said, walking to the fridge, taking out an apple, then placing it on her plate. "Here you go."

She made a face.

Matt descended the stairs with one shirt button still undone, humming a tune, and warmth spread through me as I looked at him. He smiled at me, and I asked, "Pancake, dear?" He leaned down to kiss my forehead softly before replying, "Don't mind if I do."

I grabbed a pan from the countertop and flipped a golden pancake onto a plate for him. He devoured it in delight. When Alex had finished his bacon and eggs, he requested a pancake. As I placed it in front of him, he paused and looked up into my eyes, his expression taking on a concerned intensity.

"Mom, have you found Thomas's mom yet?" he asked, his eyes wide with concern. "He must really miss her."

My heart dropped, seeing this worry in him. I knew he loved Thomas dearly. He was his best friend. I turned to face him, my hand still flipping the bacon in the pan. "No, not yet," I replied. "But I'm working on it."

Alex's face softened with understanding. "I know you can do

it, Mom, " he said, his voice filled with confidence. "If anyone can, it's you."

A warm wave of emotion flooded my heart. I looked at each of them, especially Alex, with his trusting eyes and bright smile, and was filled with a sense of power. Everything I did was for them, and it gave me the strength to take on anything.

My lips curved, and my chin dipped as I kissed him on top of his head. I could see the bright yellow school bus through the window, already stopped at the neighbor's house. The children were outside, running and shouting, their backpacks bouncing against their backs.

"You have to go! Quickly, grab your bag and lunch!" I said, gently pushing him out the door.

"Bye, Mommy," he yelled, then stormed out the door.

I stared out the window, watching as he scrambled across the street toward the bus. The driver spotted him just in time, slowing to a stop before stretching his hand over and opening the doors for him. I let out a deep sigh of relief, pouring myself a cup of coffee and leaning back against the kitchen counter. Christine and Elijah grabbed their backpacks and hopped on their bikes while Matt retreated up the stairs. Taking out my phone from my pocket, I scrolled through my emails and saw that I had finally received some information about the woman who denied knowing Rachel but called her late at night—Elyse Winters. She lived in Jacksonville, where Rachel's dad was serving time.

A thought raced through my head as I pondered what it all meant when suddenly, my phone started ringing. It was the chief.

"You need to get to Manatee Lane—the storage units down by the river. They found something."

Chapter 19

THEN:

Emma was on her knees, scrubbing the wooden floor of her bedroom with a fervor that bordered on obsession. She had to make sure everything was perfect, down to the last detail, or else her mother would be disappointed. Emma couldn't bear the thought of her mother being disappointed in her.

As she worked, she tried to push away the nagging feeling in the back of her mind. She knew she shouldn't be biting her nails, but it was a habit she couldn't seem to break. She had tried everything from wearing bitter-tasting nail polish to snapping a rubber band on her wrist every time she caught herself nibbling, but nothing worked.

Suddenly, she heard a knock on the door and her mother's voice calling out to her. "Emma, honey, can I come in?"

Emma's heart raced as she scrambled to her feet, dusting off her hands and looking around the room one last time. Everything looked perfect. Nothing was out of place; nothing was untidy. Taking a deep breath, she turned to face the door and replied, "Of course, Mom. Come in."

Her mother opened the door and stepped inside, looking around with a critical eye. Emma held her breath, waiting for her mother's approval.

"Well done, honey," her mother said, nodding. "You've really outdone yourself this time. Everything looks so clean and tidy."

Emma breathed a sigh of relief, her shoulders relaxing. She had done it. She had made her mother proud.

But her relief was short-lived. As her mother continued to inspect the room, she frowned and turned to face Emma. "What's this?" she asked, pointing at a small lock of hair on the floor.

Emma's heart sank as she saw the imperfection. She had missed it in her cleaning frenzy.

"I-I'm sorry, Mom," she stammered. "I must have missed it. I can fix it right away."

Her mother shook her head, disappointment etched across her face. "No, Emma, this isn't good enough. You need to be more thorough. You can't let something like this slip through the cracks. It's unacceptable."

Emma felt a knot form in her stomach. She had tried her best. She had done everything she could. But it was never enough for her mother.

"I'll do better, Mom," Emma said, her voice barely above a whisper. "I promise."

Her mother sighed and placed a hand on Emma's shoulder. "I know you will, honey. You're a good girl, but you need to understand that, in this family, we strive for excellence. We don't settle for anything less."

Emma nodded, and without noticing it, she started to bite her nails.

"What are you doing?" her mother exclaimed with a shriek.

Emma looked down at her hands and saw that her fingers were in her mouth again, her teeth gnawing away at her nails. She felt a hot flush spread across her cheeks as she hurriedly pulled her fingers out of her mouth and hid her hands behind her back.

"I-I'm sorry, Mom. I don't know why I keep doing that. I'll stop; I promise."

Her mother's eyes narrowed. "You know better, Emma. That's a disgusting habit."

Emma's face flushed with embarrassment. She knew her mother was right—biting her nails was a bad habit. She had tried many times to stop, but it seemed like the more she tried to resist, the more she craved it.

Her mother sighed and shook her head.

"Come here," she said in a stern voice. Emma hesitated, but the look in her mother's eyes made her do as she was told. She followed her into the kitchen and watched her mother open a drawer and remove a needle.

"What are you doing, Mom?" Emma asked nervously, backing away from the needle in her mother's hand.

Her mother ignored the question and grabbed Emma's fingers, pushing them out straight in front of her. Then she proceeded to poke the needle underneath each and every nail until they all bled.

"This is your punishment," she said firmly as she finished. "If you ever bite your nails again, I will do it again. In a week, I will check your nails; if you have been biting them, it will happen again."

Emma felt tears pricking at her eyes as she looked down at her bloody fingertips. She had never felt so embarrassed or ashamed in all her life. She started to cry helplessly, hoping to wake her mother's love and care and for her to see how crushed she was. But her mother just turned her back on her. Emma's mother walked into the kitchen and started preparing dinner, humming softly to herself. Emma followed her into the room and stood silently on the other side of the counter as she watched her mother work. She wiped her tears away, thinking this was no time to feel sorry for herself. She had failed her mother again. She knew she needed to try harder. She had to be more perfect. She simply had to.

Chapter 20

I could see the flashing lights of police cars reflecting off the yellow walls of the storage units. The area was blocked off with yellow tape, and police cars were scattered throughout the lot. As soon as I stepped out of my car, the stench hit me like a wall. I gagged and covered my nose and mouth with my shirt, trying to control my breathing. An officer flagged me down and asked for my identification before leading me toward the unit where the body was found.

I stepped closer, and the smell hit me like a ton of bricks. It was the stench of death intermingled with an odd, acrid smell. The police officers blocking off the area looked up at me as I approached, their expressions grim.

"It was in a barrel," one of them said, gesturing toward the body. "Filled with formaldehyde. Someone went to a lot of trouble to keep it preserved."

I felt a wave of nausea wash over me as I imagined the killer carefully placing the body in the barrel, sealing it shut, and adding the formaldehyde to keep it from decaying.

"But something must have gone wrong," I continued. "Something tipped the barrel over?"

I looked around and saw stray cats gathered in the grass next to us. Plates of food had been left out for them.

"Could have been a cat or a raccoon," I said, looking up toward the ceiling. "One might have gotten in here, maybe through those big vents up there, then tipped the barrel over, and the formaldehyde started leaking out underneath the door."

"When we got here, the body was lying on the ground," the officer said. "The tarp was half covering it, the barrel tipped over. The body was half in the barrel, half on the concrete floor."

As I stepped closer, I could see the outline of the body inside the barrel. It was twisted and contorted like it was trying to escape. But it was too late for that. The formaldehyde had done its job, preserving the body like a macabre work of art. I couldn't help but wonder who could have done something like this and why. But I did know who she was—the woman in the barrel, and it broke my heart.

"Her name is Rachel Baker," I said with an exhale, pushing back tears. "We've been looking for her. I'll notify next of kin."

A sudden noise made me turn around. A woman was yelling at one of the officers, demanding to know what was going on. She looked like a bum or a vagabond or maybe a drug addict. The officer tried to calm her down, but she kept shouting, getting more and more agitated.

"You're disturbing the cats," she yelled.

"Who is that?" I asked the officer next to me.

"Oh, her. That's Janet from another planet. She's harmless. They call her that because she talks like she's from another planet. She lives here on the storage unit grounds. The owner lets her stay in the back in her old, broken minivan. It's all overgrown with weeds, but she sleeps in there. She feeds the cats. We know her but have always just let her be. We check up on her from time to time, and the church brings her food. She's mad as a bat, they say. Lost her child in an accident and hasn't been quite normal since."

I watched Janet's wild eyes as she continued to scream, her voice hoarse and ragged. She was pointing at the officers, accusing them of disturbing the cats she cared for. I couldn't help but feel a sense of empathy toward her. She was alone, living in poverty, and experiencing a world of pain that I couldn't even imagine.

"Janet, calm down," I said softly, approaching her. "I'm FBI Agent Thomas. Can you tell me what you know about this area? Have you seen anything suspicious?"

Janet's eyes darted toward me, and for a moment, I saw a glimmer of recognition in them. She seemed to trust me, or at least her anger subsided for a moment.

"I've seen things—things I shouldn't have," she whispered, her voice shaking with emotion. "But no one listens to me. They all think I'm crazy."

"Tell me what you've seen," I said, trying to keep her calm. If she lived on the grounds, she could very well have witnessed something important.

"People always come here at odd hours, waking up me and my cats," she said. "Always pick-up trucks coming and going, coming and going. It never ends, I tell ya', it never ends. The ones who play loud music are the ones having sex in the cars."

"Have you seen anything strange within the past week or so?" I asked, wondering if I would get any information I could use from this strange woman. "Did you see who came to this unit, number 203?"

That made her break into deep laughter. It was a manic and maddening sound. "203?" Janet cackled, pointing a bony finger toward the unit. "That one there? "

"Yes. Has anyone been around it recently?"

"I've seen shadows moving around it, but I can't tell you

who," Janet said, her eyes widening. "I don't get too close to it, not with the smell and all."

"Do you think you could take me to where you saw those shadows?" I asked, trying to keep my voice soft. "It might be important for the investigation."

Janet hesitated, her eyes darting around as if weighing her options. Finally, she nodded and gestured for me to follow her.

We walked through the rows of storage units, our footsteps echoing through the empty aisles. Janet led me to the back of the lot, where an old minivan was parked, overgrown with weeds and vines. She pulled open the door and gestured for me to climb in.

I hesitated for a moment, wondering what I was getting myself into. But I couldn't shake the feeling that Janet knew something important, and I needed to find out what it was.

As I climbed into the minivan, the stench of cigarettes and urine hit me like a punch. Janet climbed in after me, and we settled in the darkness, surrounded by the musty smell of old clothes and trash. I tried not to gag as Janet shuffled through a pile of garbage, searching for something.

Finally, she pulled out an old flashlight and switched it on, casting a dim yellow glow around the tight space. She pointed the flashlight at the storage unit wall next to us and whispered, "I saw them there, moving around."

I leaned in closer, but all I could see was a row of metal doors lined up like soldiers in formation. "Which one?" I whispered.

"That one," Janet said, pointing to the middle door. "I saw shadows moving around it, in and out. Sometimes they'd stay there for hours, and sometimes they'd just come and go."

"Did you see who it was?" I asked.

"No, too dark," Janet said, her voice barely above a whisper. "But they weren't regular people. They moved differently, like they were hiding something."

Then, she began hitting herself. "No, no, no, Janet, why are you saying this stuff... uuhhh... what was it again?" she stopped and stared at me intensely. "How does the song go again?"

She began humming something, and I stared at her, struggling to understand her. Maybe she was just mad, after all?

I felt a shiver run down my spine as I left her, wondering what had been going on here. But most important of all was that I had learned that this killer might not have been alone. They could have had an accomplice. Was it possible that we were looking for more than one person?

Chapter 21

Kyla sat on the couch, her hands fidgeting in her lap while her mother paced back and forth in front of her. They had been talking for hours, but no matter what they said or did, they couldn't shake the feeling that something was wrong. Something was awfully wrong.

"He's done something, Kyla. I know he has," her mother said for the hundredth time, the frustration in her voice palpable. "Why else would he have cleaned the entire house? The police won't do anything; I just know it."

"We don't know that. I'm sure they're doing everything they can, Mom."

"Pah," she said, then continued back on the same track again. "I just don't understand why he would clean the house like that. It's like he was trying to cover something up. What if he killed her and was trying to get rid of the evidence?"

Kyla sighed, rubbing her forehead. "I don't know, Mom. Maybe he just wanted a clean house? Maybe he was trying to be nice? In case Rachel suddenly comes home."

Her mother stopped pacing and turned to her, a look of disbelief on her face. "Nice? John? Since when has he ever been 'nice'?"

"John can be nice. He's not a bad dad," Kyla said.

Her mother glared at Kyla. "Why are you suddenly defending him?"

"I'm not. I just don't want to jump to conclusions; that's all."

Her mom shook her head. "No, I'm certain that he's done something, and he's trying to cover it up. He's hurt Rachel; I just know it. He threatened me the other day when I went there. I'm telling ya', he's bad. I never liked him. I don't want him around the kids. I told the police that, but they won't do anything; they never do."

"I don't know, Mom," Kyla sighed. "I just wish we knew what to do."

Her mother let out a frustrated growl. "Well, we can't just sit here and wait for something to happen. We need to take matters into our own hands."

"What do you mean?"

"I mean, I have an idea, and you're gonna help me."

Kyla groaned. She really didn't want to. She just wanted things to go back to normal. But she knew that wasn't going to happen anytime soon.

"What kind of idea?" Kyla asked, already regretting the question.

"We're going to break into John's house," her mother said matter-of-factly.

Kyla's eyes widened in shock. "What?! No, we can't do that!"

"Why not? If the police won't help us, we have to do it ourselves."

"But breaking into someone's house is illegal!"

"Only if you get caught," her mother said with a sly grin. "Besides, we're not going to steal anything. We're just going to look around and see if we can find anything that might prove John did something to Rachel."

Kyla shook her head. "I don't know, Mom. This doesn't seem like a good idea."

"Come on, Kyla. You're always saying we should do something. Well, this is something."

"But what if we get caught?" she said, feeling frustrated, confused even. "What if John comes home unexpectedly?"

"We'll be careful. We'll make sure he's not home before we go in, and we'll be quick. I just need you to help me, Kyla. Please," her mother begged.

Kyla hesitated, unsure of what to do. This was a terrible idea, but she couldn't escape the thought that maybe her mother was right. Perhaps they needed to take matters into their own hands. She knew that cases like these often went cold and were put in the archives for years. They couldn't let that happen. They needed to know what had happened to her sister. And if John had hurt her, then there was no way they were letting him get away with it.

No way.

She took a deep breath and nodded. "Okay, fine. I'll help you."

Her mother's face lit up with relief and excitement. "Great! We'll go when he's not home."

Kyla nodded again, feeling something strange in the pit of her stomach. What were they getting into? But it was too late to back out now. They had made their decision, and they would have to live with the consequences.

Kyla's body stiffened as the sound of a familiar car engine rumbled up the driveway. Her eyes darted briefly in her mother's direction, who had gone pale and was now standing by the window. With trembling fingers, she pulled apart the slats of the blinds to try and get a glimpse of the car outside. "Oh, no," her mother breathed out, then whispered, "Oh, God, they're here. It's the police."

Kyla stood slowly, her mind racing with fear and confusion. She wanted to run away, to escape the suffocating feeling of being trapped in this nightmare. But she couldn't leave her mother behind, not when she was so scared and alone.

"Mom, it's going to be okay," Kyla said, though she didn't know if she believed it herself. "They're probably just here to ask us more questions about Rachel. Or maybe they found her, huh? How about that? Maybe she's home and happy again."

She tried to sound convincing, but she knew she wasn't. She couldn't hide how terrified she really was. But there was no running away now. She had to face whatever was coming.

The sound of the doorbell rang, and Kyla's mother jumped, startled. Kyla took a deep breath and walked toward the door, her heart pounding. She opened it slowly, revealing the female red-headed FBI agent standing on the porch. Her eyes were green and warm, round and soft. Her brow was creased, and her mouth turned downward in an expression of grief. Kyla knew instantly why she was there and that now, there was no going back. This was it.

Something had happened to Rachel.

Chapter 22

I took a deep breath and sat on the couch in the living room of Rachel's childhood home, her mother and sister sitting across from me. They were both fidgeting nervously, their eyes darting between me and the floor. The room was silent except for the sound of my own breathing. They both looked at me nervously as if they knew what I was about to say.

"Mrs. Johnson, Kyla," I began, "I'm sorry to have to tell you this, but we have found Rachel."

There was a sudden stillness in the room, a deafening silence that seemed to swallow everything. Mrs. Johnson's face twisted in agony, tears streaming down her cheeks. Kyla looked pale and sick, her shoulders shaking with the sobs she was holding back.

Their faces fell, and I could see tears forming in their eyes. Mrs. Johnson took a deep breath and clasped her hands together while Kyla stared at the floor.

"She's dead," I continued, my voice barely above a whisper. "We found her body this morning."

Mrs. Johnson let out a cry and covered her face with her hands while Kyla let out a small sob. I could see the pain and heartbreak in their eyes, and I wished there was something I could do to ease their suffering.

"I'm so sorry for your loss," I said softly, my heart breaking for them. I had a sister myself and had recently reconnected with her after years of being apart, and the thought of losing her was devastating to me. I knew this had to be rough. And losing a child? A daughter? Well, no one should ever experience that. It had to be the hardest thing in the world to go through.

"How? How did this happen?" Mrs. Johnson demanded, her voice trembling. "Where was she?"

"She was found in a storage unit on Manatee Lane. Her body had been put inside a barrel containing formaldehyde, possibly to preserve it, but we don't know for sure. But somehow, the barrel got tipped over inside the storage room, possibly by a stray cat or raccoon that found its way in there; we'll probably never know. But the formaldehyde started to run out underneath the garage door, and well... the lady renting the storage compartment next to it smelled it and then saw it. She called 9-1-1."

Mrs. Johnson let out a guttural scream, her whole body shaking with grief. Kyla wrapped her arms around her mother, holding her tightly as they both cried. I sat there quietly, giving them space to process their emotions and grieve. It was a devastating loss, and I knew nothing I could say or do would make it better.

After a few moments, Mrs. Johnson looked up at me with red, puffy eyes, "Who did this to my baby girl?" she asked, her voice filled with anger and pain.

"We don't know yet," I said. "But rest assured that we're investigating it. We'll do everything in our power to find out who's responsible."

Mrs. Johnson nodded, wiping away her tears with the back of her hand. "A-and how did she die?"

"We don't know for sure yet. The autopsy will tell."

Mrs. Johnson and Kyla stared at me in disbelief, their eyes wide with shock. I could see the pain etched in their faces, and my heart ached for them. I wished there was something more I could say or do to ease their suffering, but I knew words would never be enough.

Mrs. Johnson nodded, her face twisted in anger and grief. "I want justice for my daughter," she said firmly. "I won't rest until the person who did this is behind bars."

Kyla sniffled and wiped away her tears. "What do we do now?" she asked, her voice trembling.

"For now, I suggest you take some time to grieve and be with your family," I replied gently. "I have a couple of questions I would like to ask you now, if possible?"

Mrs. Johnson and Kyla looked at each other, nodding in agreement. "Of course," Mrs. Johnson said, "Whatever it takes to help find who did this to Rachel."

I pulled out my notebook and pen, ready to ask them a series of questions. I cleared my throat, then looked at the mother.

"I need to know where both of you were at the time of her disappearance, Monday morning between when she dropped off the kids at eight-fifteen and one o'clock when the car was found."

Mrs. Johnson took a deep breath before answering, "I was at work; I volunteer at the thrift store in South Cocoa Beach every Monday and Thursday. I get there at eight-thirty and leave at two o'clock."

I wrote it down, then looked at the sister.

"And Kyla?" I prompted.

"I was at home," Kyla replied, her voice barely above a whisper. "I had the day off."

"Was anyone with you? Anyone who can confirm that's where you were?"

"No."

"I can," her mom said. "I called her at eight-ten on my way to the thrift store to ask about the upcoming weekend. I'm hosting a dinner for some friends, and since Kyla is doing a little catering business on the side of her job as a chef, I've hired her to do the service for us. I was nervous about the menu, and whether it would all come out good enough, so I was... I guess I was bugging you about it."

Kyla nodded. "That's true."

I nodded and scribbled down notes in my notebook. This could be easily checked out since I would be able to see it in the phone records and also check the location of her cell phone at the time.

"Did Rachel have any enemies or anyone who might want to hurt her?" I asked.

Mrs. Johnson shook her head. "No, Rachel was a kind and loving person. She didn't have any enemies that we knew of."

Kyla nodded in agreement, "She was always trying to help people."

I nodded, writing down their words. Mrs. Johnson stared at me, shaking her head. "I just don't understand. Why are you talking to us? You know who you should be talking to?"

"Mom," Kyla said and gave her a look.

"What? Why can't I be honest? We all know it's him. We all think the same thing. Why are you asking us about our alibis when he's out there running around, getting away with it? You need to talk to John. Not us. He has threatened her before, and me too. We warned Rachel about him, but she was in love, you know how it is."

I nodded. "He is a person of interest," I said, "But I need to eliminate everything else too."

"That's nonsense," the mom said with a slight hiss. "He cleaned his house. He's been acting very strangely since she disappeared. He was the last person to see her, for crying out loud. He was the last person to see her alive."

I sighed. I had sent Matt to notify John at his work while I took care of the mother and sister. "And trust me, he is definitely interesting to us. But he also mentioned that Rachel had developed a drinking problem—that she was known to go on benders from time to time. Is this something you can confirm?"

Mrs. Johnson let out a small shriek of disbelief. "A drinking problem? Rachel? Now, I have never! She didn't have a drinking problem. John said that? I don't believe him. She enjoyed a glass of wine now and then, but she never had a problem with alcohol. I can assure you of that. "

Kyla nodded in agreement. "I never saw her drunk or out of control," she said.

I jotted down their responses in my notebook. Meanwhile, the mom snorted angrily and muttered under her breath. "Drinking problem. Not my Rachel. Why are we even talking about this?"

"Well, I need to get a complete picture of your daughter's behavior up until her death. If she did drink and go to bars, maybe she got in with the wrong crowd; maybe she got into the wrong truck with someone? I need to look at all the possibilities."

"Not my Rachel, no!" Mrs. Johnson said.

"Okay, thank you for your honesty," I said. "I just need to rule out all possibilities. We'll keep looking into John and anyone else who might be a suspect."

Mrs. Johnson looked at me, her eyes filled with tears. "Please, find who did this to my daughter," she pleaded. "She didn't deserve this. She was a good person."

"I will do everything I can to find out who did this," I promised, my heart breaking for her. "You have my word."

Mrs. Johnson and Kyla nodded, tears streaming down their faces. I got up from my chair, placing my notebook and pen back in my bag. "I'll be in touch," I said softly as I walked toward the door. "If you remember anything else, please don't hesitate to reach out to me."

Chapter 23

Kyla's heart was pounding as she stood in front of John and Rachel's house later in the day, her mom beside her, holding a duffel bag. She pulled out a flashlight and a pair of gloves and handed them to Kyla.

Kyla took them with shaking hands. She felt anxious. She had never done anything like this before, and the thought of breaking into someone's house made her feel sick. Her mom kept telling her it wasn't breaking in since it was her sister's home, but Kyla didn't buy into that. Besides, it didn't feel like Rachel's home. It had never felt that way.

"Are you sure this is a good idea?" she whispered to her mom as they scaled the fence and landed softly on the other side.

"Positive," her mom replied, giving her a reassuring pat on the back. "We need to find some evidence if we want to prove that he's the one responsible for what happened to your sister."

Kyla nodded, taking a deep breath to steady her nerves. They made their way to the back door, and her mom found the spare key where they knew Rachel kept it, then put it in the lock. They slipped inside, and Kyla's eyes widened at the sight of the home.

She hadn't been there in years, and they had done a lot to it. It was spacious and modern, with expensive-looking furniture and artwork lining the walls. Kyla couldn't help but feel a pang of jealousy for the life that Rachel had lived. She had everything, even children. John had never let Kyla and her mother see Rachel much and most certainly didn't invite Kyla over. If they saw one another, it was always just Rachel and her meeting at her place or having lunch somewhere. John had never liked Kyla and kept her from her sister. That was his controlling nature. Kyla had always warned her sister about him.

"Focus, Kyla," her mom whispered, snapping her out of her thoughts.

Right, Kyla thought, focusing on the task at hand. They searched the living room and then John's office. Her mom handed her a plastic bag and a pair of tweezers. Kyla stared at them, wondering how it had all come to this.

"Start with the desk," her mom instructed, pulling on a pair of gloves. "Look for any strands of hair or anything that might have his DNA on it. Look in all the drawers and behind books for anything that might have been a murder weapon. We don't know how she was killed yet, but if you find a knife with blood on it, then grab it."

Kyla nodded, her hands shaking slightly as she began to comb through the papers on the desk. She felt like a criminal, invading someone's personal space like this. But then again, John was no innocent either.

"Let's split up and search the place," her mom whispered, telling her she would go upstairs while Kyla searched the ground floor.

Kyla crept into the kitchen, her heart beating faster with each step. She felt like she was in a movie, but the stakes were all too real.

She opened every drawer and closet she could find, but there was no sign of anything usable. Her mom came back downstairs and snuck up behind her.

"Check the trash," her mom whispered.

Kyla's stomach twisted in knots as she opened the trash bin, the stench of rotting food hitting her nostrils. She rummaged through the garbage, her hands shaking as she searched for anything that could provide evidence.

Finally, her eyes landed on a pizza box with some crusts still in it.

"Grab it," her mother said.

"The crust?"

"Yes, it has DNA on it."

Kyla looked at the crust, not quite understanding what her mom wanted with it. How was that going to prove that he had killed Rachel? Still, she gingerly picked it up with gloved hands and handed it to her mom.

"Good job," her mom whispered, stuffing the crust in a plastic bag. "I forgot to check the bathroom," she said, then went back upstairs for a few minutes before coming back down. "I didn't find anything. I almost took his toothbrush, but then he would know we had been here. The crust will do. I really wanted to find hair, but he has cleaned everywhere so neatly that there is none."

"He's also almost bald, Mom."

"Yeah, I guess you're right. And there doesn't seem to be any murder weapon anywhere. Let's get out of here."

But as they turned to leave, the sight of headlights caught their attention. A car was pulling into the driveway.

Kyla's heart leaped into her throat as she watched John step out of the car. He looked up, his eyes narrowing as he spotted them in the window. Kyla froze, feeling like a deer caught in headlights. Her mom grabbed her arm and pulled her toward the back door.

"Run!" she hissed, and they sprinted toward the fence. Kyla's heart was beating so fast that she thought it might burst out of her chest. She could hear John's footsteps behind them and the sound of his angry voice shouting in the dark.

"Stop right there!" he yelled. "What the hell are you doing on my property?"

Kyla and her mom didn't answer; they just kept running. They scrambled over the fence, their feet slipping on the wet grass. Kyla could feel John's eyes on their backs as they disappeared into the night.

When they were finally a safe distance away, they collapsed onto the ground, panting and gasping for air. Kyla felt like she would be sick, but her mom just patted her on the back.

"Good job," her mom said, smiling at her. "Now, let's go home."

Kyla nodded, still trying to catch her breath. The adrenaline was still pumping through her veins, but she couldn't shake the feeling of guilt and fear. They had just broken into someone's home. Yes, it was her sister's, but still? What if they had been caught? What if they had been hurt?

It all seemed so surreal.

As they walked back to their car, Kyla couldn't help but glance back at her sister's house. She wondered what other secrets it held and what horrors had taken place within its walls. She shivered, feeling like she had stepped into a nightmare.

Chapter 24

I walked back into the police station, my heart pounding against my chest. I had gone back to the scene, talked to possible witnesses, and watched as the forensic techs did their job securing evidence. The investigation had taken a toll on me; the adrenaline rush from the crime scene had worn off, and my body was now paying the price. I dragged my feet toward the office, and I was looking forward to just sitting down and taking a break. When I walked in, I saw Matt standing by the coffee machine. He looked up, and his face lit up when he saw me. I could tell he had been worried about me, and seeing me safe and sound seemed to have lifted a weight off his shoulders.

He smiled as he saw me, and I returned the gesture, feeling my heart swell with love for him.

I felt my body slowly relax as Matt's arm enveloped me. I could feel the warmth radiating from him, and it suddenly felt like nothing else mattered in the world. All I wanted to do was be here with him and just forget about the world around us.

Forget that the world had lost a great woman, and three children had lost their mother. It felt shattering.

He gently asked me how things had looked at the storage facility, and I took a deep breath before spilling out all the details. He listened intently, never judging or interrupting me, and simply providing kind words and reassuring hugs whenever I needed them.

When I finished telling him everything, he looked at me with such understanding that it made my heart swell with emotion. We stood together silently for a few minutes before he finally pulled away and smiled warmly at me.

He handed me a steaming cup of coffee. "How are you feeling?"

I smiled gratefully at him. "I'm okay," I replied, sipping the coffee. It was exactly what I needed to perk me up. "Thanks for the coffee."

He nodded in understanding before asking me how the family had taken the news about Rachel's body being found.

I exhaled heavily as I thought back on it all. "As expected," I said sadly. "It never gets any easier, does it?"

"Probably not. John Baker didn't take it well, either. He cried helplessly. It was hard to watch, even though it felt slightly exaggerated."

He squeezed my hand sympathetically before pulling me into another hug. We held each other in silence for a few moments until his phone began to ring loudly, breaking us apart abruptly. He apologized profusely for having to take the call but promised that we'd continue talking later if that was okay with me. Of course, it was more than okay—it was exactly what my heart needed right then and there, so I nodded in agreement while he walked away with the phone pressed against his ear. He came back shortly after, putting the phone back in his pocket.

"There's a witness who says she saw Rachel's car on the side of the road as early as eight-twenty-five. But the doors weren't open, and it looked like someone was sitting inside it—two people."

"Rachel and her killer," I said. "Right before she died, probably."

"It's a pretty crowded road there. There must have been others who saw them and saw the killer take the body out of the car?"

I nodded, then said: "*If* she was murdered in the car. Yeah, we might want to talk to more drivers who regularly pass that area."

As I took a sip of my coffee, I felt his eyes on me. I looked up at him and smiled, feeling warmth in my chest.

He leaned in for a kiss, his soft lips pressing against mine. I felt the familiar warmth spread through my body, and a tingle ran down my spine. But our moment was interrupted by Chief Annie's voice echoing from her office, calling out to us.

"Okay, lovebirds, time for work."

We pulled away from each other, trying to conceal the blush on our faces.

Matt and I separated, and I took a seat at my desk. As I sat down, Chief Annie walked over.

"We've made some progress," she said with a solemn expression on her face. "We've found out who rented the storage unit where the body was found."

My heart skipped a beat, and I leaned in closer to hear what she had to say. "Who is it?" I asked, my mind racing with possibilities.

As she told me the name, I felt my stomach tie in knots as an icy chill swept through my body.

Chapter 25

THEN:

Emma sat quietly at the kitchen table, staring at the plate of cold spaghetti in front of her. Her mother had made it the night before and refused to let her have anything else for breakfast. Emma knew better than to argue with her mother, but her stomach was in knots.

Suddenly, her mother's shrill voice cut through the silence. "Emma, what's wrong with you? Why aren't you eating?"

"I'm not hungry," Emma mumbled, barely audible.

"You're not hungry? You're always hungry! Don't be ridiculous. Eat your breakfast!"

Her mother's voice rose with each word until she was practically shouting. Emma picked up her fork and twirled it around the spaghetti, but her stomach was churning so much that she couldn't bring herself to take a bite.

Her mother leaned over her shoulder and pinched the back of her arm hard. "I said eat your breakfast, you ungrateful little brat!"

Emma let out a whimper of pain. "It hurts. Please, stop!"

"It's your own fault. Learn to behave, little girl, or else. Now, eat!"

Emma's tears started to fall into her bowl. She didn't want to eat, and she knew her mother would hit her again if she refused, but she couldn't get the spaghetti down. She pushed the plate away and burst into a full fit of sobbing.

"You need to eat something before you go to school," her mother said sharply. "Now, stop crying and eat!"

"I can't," Emma mumbled, wiping her eyes with her sleeve.

"What did you say to me?"

"I said I can't eat it!"

"What do you mean you can't eat it? You're just being a spoiled brat and giving me a hard time!"

"I can't...."

"Just eat it!"

Her mother's voice echoed through her head, screaming at her to eat. She gritted her teeth and tried to hold back the tears, but they kept coming. As she cried, Emma thought about her favorite stuffed bunny rabbit and how, when she told her mother it was missing, she'd yelled at her for lying and hadn't believed her.

Emma felt like her whole world was crashing down around her, but she knew she had to do as her mother said. So, she brushed the tears out of her eyes and started to eat; the food seemed to be growing in her mouth and blocking her throat.

Meanwhile, her mother was pacing back and forth, ranting about how Emma was always wasting time and never doing anything useful. "You're lazy and stupid, just like your father," she spat out, her eyes flashing with anger.

Emma's eyes welled up with tears again as her mother's harsh words echoed through the house. She had always known her mother could be controlling, but lately, it seemed like she was getting worse. Emma tried to speak up, but her mother's angry voice drowned out her words.

Emma's face was pale, her eyes wide and fearful as she tried to explain herself. But with every word she spoke, her mother seemed to grow angrier. Her voice rose steadily until it filled the room like a thunderclap, drowning out Emma's quivering attempts at a rebuttal. Tears spilled down her cheeks as her mother's hand, cold and unforgiving, shot out, and her sharp nails dug into her arm. Pain bloomed across Emma's skin as her mother dug her nails into her flesh. The pain cut through Emma like a blade; she knew there would be a bruise. She knew there would be questions asked in school about this bruise. And she knew she would once again have to lie and say it was her cat or her younger sister who had done it—by accident, of course. It was always an accident. No one meant to harm her. Of course not. Whatever she did, she had to protect her secret; she had to keep the family together.

The pain from the nails digging into her skin shocked Emma, and tears began to stream down her cheeks. She tried to wipe them away, but her mother just sneered at her.

"Crying won't solve anything," she said coldly. "You need to toughen up if you want to survive in this world."

Emma bit back a cry of pain, but tears continued to stream down her face as she stumbled back.

Emma felt like she was suffocating under her mother's words. She felt like she literally couldn't breathe. She wanted to run away and never come back. She had thought about it but knew she couldn't leave her sisters behind. Her sisters were too young to understand and too little to defend themselves.

Emma felt a wave of numbness wash over her as she watched her mother turn away from her and focus her attention on her younger sister, Lily, who had just spilled a glass of milk on the table. Lily gasped and looked at her mother, eyes wide with fear. Their mother's expression hardened with a mix of anger and disappointment, and her voice rose with each word that came out of her mouth. Her mother's voice was hard and sharp, the words aimed like knives. Emma saw her reach out and grab Lily by the arm with such force that it made Emma wince. Her breathing quickened as rage surged through her veins, and she clenched her fists in anger, fighting the urge to intervene.

Their mother yelled and grabbed Lily by the arm, shaking her violently before yanking her hair. Emma felt rage boiling in her chest as she moved to intervene before it was too late. Emma knew she had to do something to protect her sister. She wiped her tears away and took a deep breath, summoning all the courage she had left. Her sister was crying helplessly, and Emma ran to help her. She pushed their mother hard—so hard she flew across the floor and landed on her knees.

Emma then grabbed her sister in her arms and carried her to the bathroom, where she locked the door. Panting and agitated, she held her sister in her arms while their mother pounded her fists on the door from the outside, screaming at them to open up. Now!

Part IV

Chapter 26

John frantically stuffed clothes into his bag, shoving it closed before slinging it over his shoulder. He knew he had to leave, had known it for weeks, but he couldn't shake the feeling that he was forgetting something. His heart was pounding as he made his way to the door, ready to make his escape, but just as his hand touched the doorknob, he heard it: the sound of a car engine roaring up his driveway, loud enough to make him jump.

He turned, reaching instinctively for the gun he kept hidden between the couch cushions before he realized it was a police car. And not just any police car—the one he'd been dreading. The one that meant his time was up.

He walked onto the porch and watched as the redheaded FBI agent from earlier stepped out of the car, her eyes locked onto him. She wasn't alone. The male detective, the same guy who had come to his work and told him about Rachel, was with her. He could feel the FBI agent's gaze boring into him like she knew everything about him—like she could see right through him. He was frozen, unable to move as she approached him. Her eyes were cold and calculating, and he knew he was in serious trouble.

"John, we need to talk," she said, her voice calm and authoritative. "I'm going to have to ask you to come with me."

John's heart was racing as he tried to come up with a response. He knew that he was in no position to argue, but he couldn't let himself be caught so easily. Without a word, he turned and bolted back inside, then through the kitchen toward the back door, his heart pounding. The agent was right on his heels, her footsteps echoing loudly in the big house.

John knew he couldn't outrun her forever, but he was determined to make a break for it. He burst through the back door and into the backyard, then found himself face-to-face with a steep drop as his house was on a canal. The agent was getting closer by the second, and he knew that he had to make a decision. He took a deep breath and made the leap, jumping into the murky water. He swam to the other side, climbed up on the dock of the Peterson's house, picked himself up, and started running again, adrenaline coursing through his veins.

He could hear the agent shouting on the other side of the canal, but John refused to look back. He had to get away, had to disappear before they caught him. He sprinted through the yard, dodging trees and leaping over roots. His lungs burned with exertion, but he didn't slow down. He knew they would be by the Peterson's house in a minute or so by car, and he needed to make it to the river on the other side.

Finally, after what felt like forever, he emerged from the yard across the street and found himself on the edge of Banana River. He could see a small paddleboard on the dock by the end of the yard, and he knew it was his only chance. He broke into a sprint once more and launched himself onto the paddle board, shoving off from the dock as the agent burst into the yard, her loud voice yelling.

John paddled furiously, his muscles screaming with exhaustion as he put as much distance as possible between himself and the shore. The agent was getting closer, and he could see her drawing a gun from her holster. He knew that he was running out of time.

John's heart was pounding as he paddled, his breaths coming in short gasps, his arms throbbing with pain. He could feel sweat trickling down his back, his arms shaking from the effort. But he refused to give up—not now, not when he was so close.

Suddenly, a shot rang out, and John felt a searing pain in his shoulder. He gritted his teeth, pushing through the pain as he redoubled his efforts. He could see the shore getting further and further away, and he knew that he was going to make it.

Finally, after what felt like an eternity, he reached the other side of the river. He hauled himself off the paddleboard, collapsing onto the ground in exhaustion. He could feel blood seeping through his shirt, and he knew that he needed medical attention, but he couldn't stop now. He had to keep moving.

He stumbled to his feet and looked around, trying to get his bearings. He saw a small, abandoned house, the windows boarded up with plywood, the roof crashed in, and the yard over-grown, and he knew that it was his best bet. He started running toward it, his injured shoulder throbbing with each step.

Finally, he reached the house and stumbled inside, shutting the door behind him, even though it was only on one hinge. He collapsed onto the dusty floor, panting and sweating, his heart pounding. He knew he couldn't stay here long, but he needed to catch his breath... to figure out his next move.

Chapter 27

"We searched everywhere; the dogs have been all over the area, and we have had boats out on the river, but there's no trace of him."

Matt's darkly circled eyes showed his exhaustion as he stood in the light from the street lamp. My stomach clenched with fear and frustration. We had been searching for John Baker all day with no luck. I was so angry with myself for letting this happen.

"Dang it," I said. "I can't believe we lost him!"

Matt sighed heavily and ran his hand through his hair in frustration.

"I know," he said. "But we have to keep looking. He can't have just vanished into thin air."

"Plus, he's wounded," I said. "He can't have made it far. Tell the hospitals to keep a lookout for him in case he tries to get medical attention."

"Already done."

My eyes were fixed on the inky blackness of the river's surface as I silently willed John to appear. The evidence against him was damning—he had rented the storage unit where Rachel's body had been found, and when we arrived to ask him about it, he had run away. We had searched for hours without luck, but I refused to abandon our pursuit. Every minute that passed felt like another page torn out of Rachel's family's story, a bleak conclusion I couldn't accept. I didn't know what I would do if we failed, but I needed answers, and I wasn't going to give up. I simply refused to.

"Let's try this side of the river once more," I said and began to walk.

The night seemed to be closing in around us as we walked along the riverbank, straining our eyes for any sign of John. I had seen him on the paddleboard as he paddled to the other side, and we had gone there, driving around the bend, but as we made it there, we found only the paddleboard that he had left. The dogs had found blood on the seawall where he had climbed up and a couple of footprints in the grass, but that's where the trail ended. It was like he had vanished.

Suddenly, I heard rustling in the bushes behind us.

"Did you hear that?" I whispered as I turned to face Matt. He nodded and drew his gun from its holster.

We slowly made our way toward the bushes, scanning the area for any sign of movement. As we neared the place where the sound had come from, a figure suddenly sprang out, making a run for it.

"Stop! Police!" Matt yelled, pointing his gun at the figure's retreating back.

The figure flew through the night like a ghost, leaving Matt and me in its dust. We raced through side streets, gasping for breath as we rounded corner after corner. The figure was always one step ahead, jumping over fences and scaling walls with impossible agility. Finally, we reached an apartment complex and saw a dark figure climbing its fire escape. With no time to waste, we gave chase, scaling the metal steps of the fire escape two at a time before emerging onto the rooftop.

There, we found the figure huddled in the corner, panting and afraid.

"Police, show us your hands," Matt yelled, gun pulled. "Show us your hands!"

As we approached this huddled figure, I placed a calming hand on his arm to lower the gun. He gave me a look, and I shook my head.

It wasn't John.

It was a small, skinny woman, and her slim body was shivering with fear.

I touched her shoulder, and she looked up at me, eyes wide in terror.

"Janet?" I said. "What are you doing here?"

Her lips were shivering as she held her hands to her temples. "It's that song, that stupid, annoying song."

Matt and I exchanged a look, and I shook my head while she kept humming. She wasn't well.

"It's okay. Janet. Let's take you back to your van."

She growled and then pulled away from me, then started to hit her head again.

Matt groaned, annoyed. "Let's just leave, Eva Rae. This is useless."

I looked at Janet and felt sorry for her. She seemed so tormented.

"I'm so stupid," she said. "I'm so stupid. I should have... I came to tell you something."

"Come on, Eva Rae, let's just go," Matt said.

"Wait," I said.

"You can't be serious?" he said, rolling his eyes. "You know they call her Janet from another planet for a reason, right?"

I knelt beside her. "Tell us what, Janet? What did you want to tell us?"

She stopped hitting herself and looked at me. "Not want to.

Oh, no, I definitely didn't want to. I need to. There's a difference, you know? I *need* to tell you something. The voices are telling me to."

"Okay. What do you need to tell me?" I asked.

"Geez," Matt said in the background. "This is ridiculous."

Janet looked up at him with anger.

"Don't listen to him," I said. "Focus on me, Janet. What did you need to tell us?"

"There was a thing on the ground outside of number 203 after they were there, the strange shadows—you know, the ones you asked about?"

"Yes, I remember," I said. "But what did you find?"

Her eyes looked mad as they lit up. "I found it and picked it up. It was so shiny."

"What was it, Janet? What did you find?" I asked.

"It was gold."

"Oh, here we go," Matt groaned.

"What do you mean gold?"

"Pure gold. It was beautiful."

"She found gold," Matt repeated. "We're wasting our time."

"Wait a second and give her a chance," I said. "What do you mean you found gold? Can you show it to me?"

She stared at me, then shook her head. "Wait a second." she reached into the pocket of her dirty hoodie and pulled something out. She held it up to me with a smile. I looked down and saw it.

"This one. This is it."

It was a gold necklace with initials on it.

J.B.

John Baker.

Chapter 28

David Parker had been planning his escape for days. He had studied the prison layout, memorized guard schedules, and calculated every possible risk. And now, finally, the moment had arrived.

He made his way to the exercise yard, heart pounding. It was a clear day, the sun shining down on the concrete walls surrounding him. The other inmates were scattered throughout the yard, some playing basketball, others lifting weights. David tried to keep his movements casual, blending into the background.

As he approached the wall, he looked up and down, left and right, making sure no one was watching. Then, with a deep breath, he placed his hands and feet on either side and started to crab-walk up.

It was slow going at first, the narrow space between the walls barely allowing him enough room to move. But as he climbed higher, he started to gain speed. He could feel the air rushing past him, the exhilaration of freedom so close he could almost taste it.

David Parker's heart pounded as he crawled into the narrow

space between the two walls. He could feel the rough edges scraping against his skin as he crab-walked up, inch by inch. His muscles ached with the effort, but he knew he couldn't afford to stop.

Finally, he reached the top and peered over the edge. The exercise yard was empty now as all the prisoners were getting back inside, and he could hear the guards laughing and joking in the distance. He knew it was only a matter of minutes, if not seconds, before they'd realize he wasn't among them. He took a deep breath and pushed himself up, his hands gripping the edge as he pulled himself over.

He landed on the roof with a soft thud and paused for a moment, catching his breath. The wind was picking up, the air cool against his skin. He could see the fence in the distance, the razor wire glinting in the sunlight.

David dug the toes of his shoes into the rough, tar-covered roof and felt the thrill of freedom as his feet pounded against it. His heart raced with adrenaline as he ran faster and faster until he reached the metal fence. With a burst of strength, he leaped up and hoisted himself over it just as the guards' angry shouts filled the air.

The fence was covered in razor wire, and David knew that if he touched it, he would be severely injured. But he had no choice. He pushed himself through the wire, feeling the sharp blades cutting into his skin, but the adrenaline kept him going.

Finally, he made it through and dropped down to the ground on the other side. He ran as fast as he could, knowing the guards were behind him, their angry shouts filling the air. He could hear the sound of barking dogs and the crackle of their radios. They were closing in on him fast.

David darted through the trees, dodging branches and jumping over fallen logs. He could feel the sweat pouring down his face and his heart pounding in his chest. He had to find a way to lose them, to disappear. David had always known that escaping from prison was risky, but he had no other choice. He had been framed for a crime he didn't commit, and he couldn't spend the rest of his life in a cell. He had to clear his name, which meant taking matters into his own hands.

He could hear the sirens in the distance, but he didn't care. All that mattered was getting as far away from the prison as possible. He needed an escape.

Finally, he saw it. A car parked on the side of the road, engine running. He ran toward it, his legs pumping with exertion. As he got closer, he realized the driver was a woman, her blonde hair pulled back into a tight ponytail.

Without hesitation, David jumped into the passenger seat and slammed the door shut.

"Drive!" he shouted, his voice hoarse with emotion.

The woman looked at him in surprise, but as their eyes met, she didn't hesitate. She put her foot on the gas, and the car shot forward, leaving a cloud of dust in its wake. David leaned back in his seat, his heart still racing with adrenaline and his body thrumming with anticipation.

"Who are you?" the woman asked, glancing over at him. "What the hell is going on?"

"I'm David," he replied, his voice still breathless. "And I just broke out of prison."

The woman's eyes widened in shock, but she didn't slow down. "Well, shit," she muttered. "I guess we're in this together now."

David couldn't help but grin. He had no idea who this woman was, but he knew she was his ticket to freedom. They drove in silence for a few minutes, the sound of the sirens fading into the distance.

"So, where are we going?" the woman asked, glancing over at him again.

David hesitated for a moment, wondering how much he should tell her. But he knew that he needed her help if he was to reach his destination. His face would be everywhere soon.

"Cocoa Beach," he said. "I need to get there as soon as possible. Don't worry about the cost. I got some money stashed away. I will pay you for this."

She hit the accelerator hard, and they jolted forward.

"You had me at money."

Chapter 29

Wput out a search everywhere for John Baker. Chief Annie went on TV and asked the public for help, telling them to look at their Ring cameras and let us know if anything suspicious showed up in the area and if anyone might have seen him. It was a race against time to find John Baker, and every minute that passed made our task more daunting. As we canvassed the area the next day, knocking on doors and speaking with residents, we found little to go on.

"He has a brother," I said while Matt and I were sitting at the station, frustrated, researching John Baker's background, trying to figure out where he might have gone.

"Really?" Matt said.

"Yeah, his name is Mike. I found a picture of them together on John's Facebook page. It looks like they were pretty close," I replied, scrolling through John's social media profiles.

"Okay, let's see if we can find Mike's contact information and talk to him. Maybe he knows something that can help us find John," Matt suggested.

We spent the next hour digging through online records and

eventually found Mike's address and phone number. Matt called him while I prepared to go to his house and speak with him in person. He lived in Cape Canaveral, so it wasn't far away.

We drove to Mike Baker's house, which was a small, rundown place with peeling paint and a rusted mailbox. We knocked on the door, and after a few moments, it opened to reveal a scruffy-looking man in his thirties with piercing blue eyes and a crooked smile.

"Can I help you?" he asked, eyeing us suspiciously.

"We're looking for your brother, John Baker," I said, showing him our badges. "Do you know where he is?"

Mike's face clouded over. "No, I haven't seen him."

"Can we come in? And have a talk?"

He thought it over for a few seconds, then let us in. The pungent smell of beer hit me as soon as we entered the house. The room was dimly lit, with empty beer bottles scattered everywhere. The living room was cluttered with beer cans, empty pizza boxes, and old magazines. Mike gestured to a couch, and we sat down.

"Look, I don't know anything about John," he said, avoiding our gaze.

"Come on, Mike, we know you're lying. You two are brothers. You must know something," Matt said firmly.

Mike sighed and took another swig of beer. "Okay, fine. Something has been troubling me since all this began—since Rachel disappeared."

"And that is?" I asked.

He gave me a look, and I understood this wasn't easy for him. This felt like a betrayal.

"He said something last time we were together," he said. "I found it strange but pushed it to the back of my mind at first, but then Rachel went missing, and I...." He paused and sighed, running a hand through his stubble. "I don't know; maybe it's nothing."

"What did he say?" Matt asked. "It might be useful to us."

"I don't want to get him in trouble if...."

"He's already in trouble," I said. "Running from the police is considered an admission of guilt, in case you don't know it."

He exhaled and leaned forward, resting his elbows on his knees. "I always liked Rachel, and to know that something happened, that she was killed, it breaks my heart. My brother... I don't know if he is capable of something like this, but he said stuff, you know?"

"What did he say?" I asked.

He looked up at me, eyes sorrowful. "He said that he wished she was gone. On the day before she disappeared."

"And what was the context?" I asked. "What were you two talking about?"

"We were having a beer here at my place and just having our usual banter when he suddenly grew very serious and started to talk about his marriage and said he wasn't sure they'd make it. He said it was so bad that he just wished she was gone. That's how he said it. And the way he said it—like he really meant it—and for a second, I remember thinking it was strange the way he looked at me like he had already made up his mind—like he had planned to do something. When he left, I couldn't stop thinking about it, but I just told myself I was crazy. He's my brother. I should know that he isn't capable of something like that."

"But you have your doubts," I said. "Or you wouldn't be telling us this."

He nodded, biting the inside of his cheek. "You're right. You're very right."

"Do you have any idea where he might be hiding?" Matt asked. "Has he contacted you?"

Mike shook his head. "No. Not a sound. I was expecting him to, but so far, he hasn't."

"Well, if he does, please let us know," I said, handing him my card. "And please tell him to turn himself in. There's nowhere he can hide."

Mike nodded again.

"Oh, and another thing," I said, pulling out my phone. I showed him a picture of the necklace that Janet had found.

"Is this his? Do you know?"

Mike looked at the picture and then sighed. "It belonged to our father. His name was also John Baker. When our dad died, John wanted to have it. It had sentimental value for him, he said."

"Thank you," I said. "I know it can't be easy to tell us these things. But you did the right thing."

Mike's eyes glistened with unshed tears, and he nodded in acknowledgment. "I just want Rachel's family to have closure. And if John had something to do with it, I want him to pay for what he's done."

"We'll do everything we can to find him," I assured him. "And if he has nothing to hide, he should turn himself in and clear his name."

Mike nodded in agreement and showed us to the door. As we walked back to our car, I couldn't shake the feeling that there was more to this story than we knew. John Baker was still out there, and the clock was ticking. We needed to find him—soon.

Chapter 30

THEN:

Emma could barely breathe as she hugged her sister tightly, the sound of their mother's pounding on the door only making her heart race faster. She had never been so terrified in her life.

"Emma, what are we going to do?" her sister whispered, tears streaming down her face.

"I don't know," Emma whispered back, feeling helpless. She tried to think of a way out, but all she could hear was the sound of their mother's voice screaming for them to open the door.

The pounding on the door grew louder, and Emma could feel the wood shaking under the force of her mother's rage.

"Open this door right now!" their mother shouted.

Emma knew they couldn't keep the door locked forever. She had to think of something, anything, to get them out of this situation.

Emma held her sister tightly as they huddled together in the cramped bathroom. The sound of their mother's fists pounding against the wooden door reverberated through the small space, making Emma's heart race with fear. She could hear her sister's sobs and knew that she had to be strong for both of them.

"Girls, open this door right now!" their mother shouted, her fists hitting against the wood.

"It's going to be okay," Emma whispered, brushing a strand of hair from her sister's tear-stained face.

Emma's heart raced as she tried to calm her sister. She knew their mother's rage was unpredictable and explosive. She never knew what would set her off next.

"What are we going to do, Emma?" her sister whispered through her sobs. "She's going to hurt us."

Emma's mind raced as she tried to come up with a plan. She knew they couldn't stay in the bathroom forever. But she couldn't bear the thought of going back out there where their mother waited.

"Listen to me," Emma said, her voice firm. "We're going to wait in here until she calms down. And then, we're...."

But as the pounding grew louder and more insistent, Emma began to doubt her own words. She knew their mother could be unpredictable at times, and she feared what might happen if she forced her way into the bathroom.

Emma tried to distract her sister by talking about anything that came to mind. They talked about their favorite movies, their dreams for the future, and even about their childhood memories. But as the minutes stretched on, the pounding continued, and the girls began to feel trapped.

Scared and alone.

As Emma looked around the small bathroom, her eyes landed on the window. It was a small, narrow window, but it seemed like their only way out.

Emma's eyes widened as she realized what she had to do. She quickly got up and walked toward the window, her heart racing with fear.

"What are you doing?" her sister asked, looking at her with confusion and worry.

"I have an idea," Emma said, her voice shaking slightly. "We're going to climb out the window."

Her sister's eyes widened with fear, and she shook her head. "I can't do that. I'm too scared."

"We don't have a choice," Emma said, her voice firm. "We have to get out of here."

Emma started climbing onto the toilet seat and then onto the bathtub's edge. She reached up and unlatched the window, then pushed it open as far as it would go. The warm air rushed in, and Emma took a deep breath, feeling a sense of freedom for the first time in hours.

She turned to her sister. "Come on, follow me."

The sound of their mother's pounding grew louder as Emma hoisted herself up and squeezed through the narrow opening, her heart racing with fear. She helped her sister through the window, and they climbed out onto the house's roof.

Emma's heart raced as they made their way across the slanted roof. She could feel the shingles cutting into her bare feet as she tried to keep her balance. Her sister followed closely behind, tears still streaming down her face.

As they neared the edge of the roof, Emma felt a rush of fear and adrenaline overcome her. It was a long way down, and she didn't know if they would make it, but she knew they had to try.

"Jump," Emma whispered to her sister. "Take my hand."

Her sister hesitated for a moment before nodding and jumping off the roof. Emma caught her hand effortlessly, and they both tumbled to the ground below, landing with a soft thud.

As they ran away from their mother's rage, Emma knew their lives would never be the same again. But for the first time in a long time, she felt a glimmer of hope.

Chapter 31

The real estate agent's car pulled up slowly in front of the house, the wheels crunching over the gravel driveway. He parked the car and turned to face his clients, a young couple in their early thirties. The wife was heavily pregnant, her hand resting protectively over her swollen belly. The husband looked hesitant, eyeing the worn-out house with a critical gaze.

"This property is a diamond in the rough," the agent said, stepping out of the car and walking toward the couple. "But with a little TLC, it could be a wonderful home for you and your coming children."

The wife looked up at her husband, a glimmer of hope in her eyes. He took her hand, giving it a reassuring squeeze before turning back to the agent.

"What kind of work are we talking about here?" he asked, eyeing the house's peeling paint and cracked windows. "It looks like a lot. We don't really have money or time for that."

"Just some cosmetic stuff," the agent replied. "New paint, new windows, maybe some landscaping. But let me show you the potential."

With that, he led the couple toward the house. The wife's eyes scanned the house's exterior, probably imagining a small garden outside with some roses and maybe a swing set. Her husband's mind was definitely running wild with ideas, "Maybe a tree house over there?" he said, pointing to the corner of the yard.

As they walked closer to the front door, the agent continued to extol the virtues of the property. "The roof was redone last year, and the plumbing and electrical were all updated in the past five years. It's got good bones."

The couple exchanged a glance that said they were both thinking the same thing. They saw the potential in the house, and the agent's words had given them renewed hope. The agent found the key and put it in the lock. The door creaked open, revealing a dusty and outdated interior. The husband's face fell slightly, but the wife's eyes sparkled with imagination.

"We could knock down this wall here," she said, gesturing toward the living room. "Open up the space and let in more light."

The agent nodded, impressed by her vision. "That's exactly the kind of thing I'm talking about," he said with a grin. "This is such a great neighborhood, and you can get this within your price range. Fix it up, and it will be worth a lot more. Let's take a closer look."

With that, the three of them stepped further inside the house, the pregnant wife leading the way. Her husband was trailing behind but seemed more interested. The three of them continued to explore the house, with the agent pointing out the potential in each room. The wife's mind was racing with ideas, picturing the perfect nursery for their baby and a cozy living room for family movie nights. Her husband was starting to come around, seeing the possibilities in each room as they walked through.

As they stepped outside, the couple looked back at the house with newfound optimism. They could see the potential the real estate agent had described, and they were starting to believe this could be their dream home. The wife squeezed her husband's hand, a silent affirmation that they were in this together.

"We'll put a bid in," the husband said firmly, looking at the agent with a new sense of determination.

The agent grinned, feeling a sense of satisfaction. He knew this couple was going to turn this house into something special, and he was happy for them and their family. That was the best part of being a real estate agent: helping people find the homes that fit their needs. A beautiful family would live here, and the children would grow up and one day leave. It was such a wonderful thing to be able to help them with.

"And the schools here are excellent, by the way," he added.

The couple both smiled in awe at this little gem they had found. They truly were lucky.

"Oh, wait, I almost forgot, the real estate agent said, holding a finger in the air. "The cabin in the back."

He began walking to the back door, and they followed him. "It's this cute little thing set down by the river banks. It can easily be turned into a mother-in-law suite if you like. It even has plumbing. You could easily set up a small kitchen, and boom, you would have an Airbnb and create some additional income, or just let friends live there. It even has views of the river. Let me show you."

He slowly pushed his way through the waist-high grass, the family of soon-to-be three following behind. The cicadas hummed a rhythm in the humid air as the wife spotted a squirrel scurrying up an old oak tree. They stopped at the edge of a small clearing, and there before them stood a rustic cabin, its chipped paint and aging wood made even more beautiful by the hint of sunlight peeking through the branches above. It needed a new roof, but that would be easily done.

The real estate agent stepped forward and grabbed hold of the door handle; it creaked slightly as he opened it. He took one step into the room, then froze. The couple moved closer behind him, standing next to him with matching smiles on their faces—that is, until they saw what had caused him to stop suddenly.

The wife gasped; her hand flew to her mouth, and she screamed.

Chapter 32

I shuffled into the precinct, my steps echoing off the walls. As I arrived at Chief Annie's office, I heard raised voices coming from inside. Taking a deep breath, I knocked on the door.

"Come in," she said sharply. She had been on the phone and put it down.

When I entered her office, I could see her lips were pressed into a thin line, and her forehead was creased with worry. She motioned toward a chair, and without even needing to hear what was wrong, I knew it wasn't good. I feared it had to do with the fact that I hadn't been able to find John Baker. I felt like a failure.

"What's going on?"

"They've found something in an abandoned house in Snug Harbor in the south part of town," she said, her voice low. "I need you and Matt to go check it out."

I stared at her, surprised. "What did they find?"

"A body. That's all I know. Some real estate agent was about to show the house to his clients and found him inside the back cabin."

I could feel the adrenaline already coursing through my veins.

I stood up and left her office, ready to race to the scene. As I left, I could hear Chief Annie's final words ringing in my ears.

"Be careful, and call for backup if you need it."

I didn't waste any time. I told Matt to come with me, and we hurried to my car and sped off toward Snug Harbor. When we arrived, I saw police cars and officers swarming around the abandoned house. I quickly parked and hurried across the yard toward the small cabin in the back. Matt came rushing behind me.

My heart sank as I saw the blood on the floor. It was everywhere, staining the wooden boards a deep crimson. As I stepped closer, I could see the handprints and smears where someone had tried to crawl away. I could feel the weight of the situation threatening to pull me under, but I pushed it aside.

I lifted my gaze and saw the stretcher being wheeled out, a man lying on it. My heart stopped as I recognized him.

It was John Baker. He was still alive, someone told me, as they rushed him out the door and into the ambulance.

I watched the ambulance pull away, sirens blaring as it raced toward the hospital. My mind was racing with questions.

But there was one thought that stood out above all the rest. I hoped he survived. Not because I cared about him but because I wanted him to pay for what he did to his wife.

Rachel was my friend, and seeing what John did to her broke my heart. They had children together, young ones who would miss their mother terribly and never recover from losing her. She had been so full of life, so full of hope and ambition. But John had taken all that away from her.

I knew that if John survived, he would have to face the consequences of his actions. He would have to stand trial for what he did to Rachel. I was going to make sure of it. And I wanted to be there to see it happen.

As I stood there, watching the police gather evidence and the paramedics pack up their equipment, I couldn't help but feel a sense of satisfaction. We got him. John Baker was caught, and justice would be served. It may not bring Rachel back, but it was a small comfort to know that her killer would face the punishment he deserved.

I turned to leave the abandoned house, my mind still reeling from what I had seen. But as I stepped out into the sunlight, I couldn't help but feel a sense of relief. Relief that John Baker was still alive. Relief that he would face trial for his crimes. And relief that Rachel's memory would be honored by his punishment.

Chapter 33

The wind howled outside, and Elyse Winters looked worrisomely at the window, then sighed.

"Continue, Mommy, why did you stop?" her son Charlie said.

She looked at her boy, then smiled gently. Then, she continued to read the story. It was already the third book, and she had told him it was the last one of the night, and then it was time to sleep. Her phone lit up, warning of a severe thunderstorm approaching, and she could hear the thunder rumbling in the distance as it slowly grew closer to her small mobile home. She could feel the tension building inside her but tried to shake it and focus on tucking in her son. Lightning flashed nearby, lighting up the entire room, and she jumped, startling her son.

"Sorry, my love," she whispered, giving him a reassuring smile and kissing the top of his head. "Mommy is a little on edge lately."

"You're silly," her son laughed. "It's just lightning and thunder."

"You're right," she said with a light chuckle. It really was silly to be so worried about a thunderstorm. It wasn't so much the storm itself that worried her; it was the risk of tornadoes being born inside it. The mobile home they lived in would not be able to withstand a tornado should one be created, as they were from time to time in Florida. She wished she could afford a real house for her and her son, but being a single mom, she didn't have the money for it.

It will be okay. At least you're safe.

As she finished the story and kissed her son goodnight, she couldn't shake the feeling that she was being watched. The hairs on the back of her neck stood up, and she scanned the room, but nothing was out of place.

She was being silly again.

"Good night, my love," she said and turned off the lights. She left, leaving the door slightly open as Charlie preferred it. She sighed as she headed to the living room, her head filled with worries about the future. She sat on the couch just as another thunderclap rumbled through, startling her again. She turned on the TV for some distraction. But she could still hear the strong gusts of wind as they howled outside, and she shivered. She pulled her blanket tighter around her. As she began to watch her show, a sudden bolt of lightning illuminated the room, casting eerie shadows on the walls. Elyse jumped again, her heart racing with fear. She turned to look out the window, hoping that the storm would blow over quickly.

As she reached the end of the newest episode of *Below Deck*, there was a sudden knock at the door. She jumped, startled by the sudden noise. She hesitantly made her way to the door, peering through the peephole to see who was there.

But there was no one there.

"It's just your imagination," she whispered to herself. "Just you being silly mommy again, Elyse."

She looked once more to be sure, but no one was out there— just the palm trees swaying in the strong winds. Anxiety grew inside her, but she decided it was just the wind playing tricks on her. It had to be. Then she decided to go to bed. Maybe she would be able to sleep through the storm. She made her way back toward her bedroom, but as she walked down the dark hallway, she heard a noise behind her. It was faint at first, but it grew louder with each step she took. Her heart pounding, she tried to convince herself it was just the wind, but she knew deep down it wasn't.

She reached her bedroom door, her hand shaking as she reached for the doorknob. Then she heard the noise again. Turning around, she saw a figure in the shadows. It was too late for her to react. She gasped and tried to scream, but a hand clamped over her mouth, muffling her cries.

"You think you can leave?" the voice behind the dark shadow said. "Only death can part us."

Chapter 34

I sat at the dinner table, the chair screeching across the tiles. I felt happy, really happy. For once, we were all gathered—all my four children and Matt and Elijah—the entire family.

My family.

Outside, the clouds had turned dark as another thunderstorm approached. As we sat around the dinner table, the smell of freshly baked lasagna was wafting through the air. I looked around and smiled at my beautiful children, who threw themselves at the food.

"So, how was everyone's day today?" I asked.

Angel threw a handful of lasagna on the floor, her chubby hands covered in tomato sauce, while Alex was frowning at his plate, pushing his food around with his fork.

No one answered. The teenagers grumbled and shoved food down their throats like they hadn't been fed in weeks, and then they asked to be excused and rushed upstairs to their rooms before I could even answer.

It was okay. I was used to it. They were so busy with their lives. Only Angel and Alex remained.

"So, how was your day?" I asked, trying to engage them in conversation.

Angel responded by giggling and kicking her feet under the table while Alex looked up at me with his big brown eyes. I sensed something was coming, and it did.

"Mom, is it true that Thomas's mom is dead?" he asked, his voice barely above a whisper.

I felt a lump form in my throat. I hesitated momentarily, unsure if I should tell him the truth. But I decided to be honest. He would hear it somehow anyway. It was bound to be something they'd talk about in school.

"Yes, Alex, that's true," I replied, trying to keep my voice steady.

Alex's face fell as he looked down at his plate. I could see the sadness in his eyes, and I wished I could shield him from the world's harsh realities. Alex's face darkened.

"But why, Mom?" he asked, his voice shaking.

I sighed, wondering how much to tell him. I didn't want to burden my son with the horrible things that could happen in life, not when he was so young. But I knew that I had to be truthful with him.

"I'm sorry, Alex," I said, reaching out to touch his hand.

Oblivious to the somber conversation, Angel continued throwing more food on the floor while humming to herself. Alex remained silent for a few moments, his eyes clouded with sadness. I reached over and gave his hand a gentle squeeze, hoping to offer some comfort.

"It's so sad," Alex said, finally breaking the silence.

I nodded in agreement, feeling a pang of sadness in my chest. "It is, Alex, but we have to be strong for Thomas and his family. They need our support right now."

Alex nodded solemnly, and Angel continued to play with her food. She was still throwing it on the floor and laughing.

"Angel, please stop," I said, trying to keep my composure.

"Will Thomas be okay?" Alex asked.

"I don't know," I said, evading the truth of Thomas's father's situation. It was too much to handle for a child of his age, knowing that his father would soon go to jail.

I felt more sadness wash over me. It was a tragic situation, and three children had lost their mother and father in one stroke. I couldn't imagine what they were going through.

I tried to lighten the mood by changing the subject, "So, Angel, did you have fun at daycare today?"

Angel nodded her head vigorously, food still smeared all over her face. I couldn't help but smile at her innocence.

Once the kids were done and went to the living room, Matt grabbed a beer from the fridge, and I opened a bottle of Chardonnay. We raised our glasses to the fact that we had finally caught our killer. As I sipped my wine, I couldn't help but feel a twinge of guilt. Yes, we had caught the killer, but at what cost? Three children were now left without parents and a family torn apart by tragedy.

And where were those children now? Only John knew.

I looked over at Matt, who looked pensive as well. I knew he was thinking about the same thing I was. We had been so focused on catching John Baker that we had forgotten about the innocent victims. We clinked our glasses together, both lost in our own thoughts.

But I promised myself that I would do everything in my power to help those children. They had lost so much already, and I couldn't bear the thought of them suffering any more than they already had. They still had family here and would be able to be with them as soon as we found them.

As the storm raged outside, I sat there with Matt, sipping our drinks in silence. It was a bittersweet moment, but for now, it was enough to know that justice would be served.

Chapter 35

THEN:

Emma and Lily clung to each other as they ran away from their home, their breath coming in ragged gasps as they propelled themselves forward. Lily's hand was sweaty in Emma's grasp, but neither of them dared to let go. They had walked for hours, their little legs carrying them as far away from their former life as possible.

As the last rays of light stretched across the sky, Emma noticed a run-down tunnel off to one side. Its entrance was covered in overgrown weeds and ivy, and it seemed untouched by human hands for years. She turned to Lily with determination in her eyes, grabbed her hand, and started walking toward it. They were surprised to find that the walls were still standing despite being coated in a thick layer of grime and cobwebs. The air was stale and damp, but it provided them with the perfect hiding place from their troubles. It was dark and foreboding, but she didn't hesitate to lead Lily into it. They crept inside, the murky darkness enveloping them and the distant sounds of the city fading away.

The tunnel was damp and smelled like mildew, but it gave the girls a place to hide from the world.

Lily clutched Emma's hand tightly as they stepped cautiously into the unknown. Their eyes adjusting to the dim light, they noticed a tiny pool of murky water in one corner and, without hesitation, fell to their knees, thirstily lapping it up. All around them, walls dripped with moisture, and a distant rumbling was heard echoing down the passageway. Trembling, they hugged each other close as they huddled together in the dark.

Lily clung to Emma, their small bodies shaking with fear as they crouched in the dark, humid tunnel.

"What's gonna happen to us?" Lily asked, her small voice shivering.

"I don't know," Emma said. "But at least we're safe. Don't talk. She might be looking for us and will hear us if she comes close."

As they sat in the darkness, listening to the sound of their own breathing, they both were wondering what would happen to them. Would they be found and forced to go back home? Would they be taken away by strangers who would hurt them even more?

"I'm scared," Lily finally said, ignoring her sister's comment to keep quiet. She simply couldn't hold it in anymore.

"Me too," her sister replied. She pulled Lily closer and held her in her arms.

"She might find us," Lily said.

"We will run again," Emma said. "We will keep running if we have to."

Lily went quiet and nodded her head. After a long silence, she said:

"But what about mom?"

"What about her? We're running from her."

"But will she be okay?"

"What do you mean?"

"Will she be okay without us?" Lily said, her eyes filling.

Emma felt her heart clench at the unexpected question. She knew her sister was right; their mother wouldn't be okay without them. But she also knew they couldn't go back, not after what their mother had done to them.

"We can't worry about that now," Emma finally said, trying to keep her voice from breaking. "We need to focus on staying safe and finding a way to survive."

Lily nodded, tears spilling down her cheeks. Emma wiped them away and held her tightly, both trying to find comfort in each other's embrace.

Emma held her tight, her own eyes wet with unshed tears. They sat in the darkness, two little girls trying to survive in a world that was too big and scary for them.

But they had each other, and for now, that was enough.

Part V

Chapter 36

Caroline lay in her bed, sound asleep when something woke her. Her furry companion, a golden retriever named Duke, nuzzled his head against her lap, tail wagging eagerly as he let out a low whine.

Caroline glanced down at him, groaning. "Do you need to go outside?"

Duke barked in response, jumping off her lap and running toward the door. She looked at her phone; it was five o'clock in the morning. She didn't have to get up yet.

Caroline groaned. It was too early, and she didn't want to have to walk Duke, but she also didn't want to deal with cleaning up any accidents in the house, should he have one. Duke was still a young dog and had never been very good at holding it in for longer periods of time. Reluctantly, she got up, following Duke outside in the darkness.

She stood on the back porch, letting the warm night air embrace her like a humid blanket. It was already hot out, and the sun hadn't even risen yet.

"Duke, come on," she called out into the darkness. "Let's go back inside."

But there was no response. Caroline furrowed her brow, her heart starting to race.

"Duke?" she called out again, louder this time, her voice now tinged with panic. "Duke, where are you?"

Still, there was no response. Caroline felt a knot forming in her stomach as she stepped off the porch and into the backyard, calling out for Duke once more. She walked into the yard and peered into the darkness but couldn't see anything beyond the fence surrounding her backyard.

Suddenly, she heard a sound coming from the other side of the fence, from the neighbor's backyard. It was a strange noise, like something scraping against wood. Caroline hesitated for a moment, then decided to investigate. Something about the sounds made her uneasy. She walked toward the fence, Duke's barking getting louder with each step.

"Stop it, Duke," she scolded as she peered through the slats in the fence. But Duke wouldn't listen. He dug furiously at the ground, pulling at something Caroline couldn't quite see. She walked along the fence until she reached the gate separating her yard from her neighbor's.

Duke ran toward her as she pushed the gate open, barking loudly. He then took off again. He stopped at the base of a large tree, digging frantically at the ground and pulling at something with his teeth.

"Stop it, Duke," Caroline scolded, pulling him away from the tree. "What are you doing?"

But Duke wouldn't listen. He kept growling and barking, staring intently at the spot where he had been digging. Caroline peered closer, and her heart sank. She let out a blood-curdling scream, backing away from the tree in horror. Duke continued to growl and dig, his eyes fixed on the gruesome sight before them.

He was pulling at it, biting into it, and the crunching sound made her sick.

There, buried in the ground, was a hand. It was mottled and pale, long fingers stretching upward as if pleading for help. Caroline felt bile rise in her throat as she backed away from the tree. Panicking, she stumbled back, her hand covering her mouth as she tried to hold back the vomit that threatened to spill out.

She fumbled with her phone, shaking as she dialed 9-1-1. It felt like an eternity before someone picked up on the other end.

"9-1-1, what's your emergency?" the operator asked.

"There's a body in my neighbor's backyard," Caroline blurted out, her voice shaking. "Please, you have to send someone."

The operator tried to calm her down, asking for her address and details about the situation. Caroline struggled to answer, her mind racing with fear and confusion.

She hung up the phone and looked at Duke, who was still growling and barking at the ground. She tried to pull him away, but he resisted, his teeth sinking deeper into the flesh of the hand.

Caroline felt a wave of nausea wash over her as she stumbled back, tripping over a stray tree branch and falling to the ground. She lay there for a moment, her heart pounding, before struggling to her feet and running back to her house, where she locked all the doors behind her.

Chapter 37

"Good morning, everyone," Chief Annie began, a smile spreading across her face.

I lifted my gaze and met hers as she entered the morning meeting at the police station. The room was filled with detectives and officers, all eager to hear any new information she would bring. My eyes were glued to Chief Annie as she addressed the room. Her normally stern face was lit up with a smile, and I couldn't help but feel a sense of relief wash over me.

"I'm happy to say that we have our guy. Everything points to John Baker killing his wife, Rachel Baker, and frankly, the evidence is mounting against him. Now, John is currently in the hospital, recovering from a gunshot wound, and hasn't woken up yet. But there's no doubt in my mind that he's our man. I want to applaud everyone here for working tirelessly to apprehend him, especially Agent Thomas and Detective Miller, who figured him out and chased after him when he ran. Agent Thomas was the one who shot and wounded him. He then managed to escape and took shelter in an abandoned house but had nowhere to go from there, and he was bleeding too heavily to move. That's when the real estate agent found him as he was about to show the house to potential buyers. Well done, Agent Thomas and Detective Miller."

Chief Annie paused with a satisfied smile on her lips. A round of applause erupted from the room. It was a relief to finally have a suspect in custody.

"But we still have a lot of work to do," Annie continued. "We received the autopsy report this morning, and it's not pretty. Rachel was killed by a single stab wound to the chest. The time of death is between 8:20 and 9:20 a.m. on the day she disappeared."

A hush fell over the room as we all absorbed this brutal piece of information. It was quickly replaced by a murmur of disgust and outrage that rippled through the room. I clenched my fists, feeling the anger and frustration bubbling up inside me. But I tried to stick to the facts, and this news meant she wasn't killed inside the car since that would have left blood stains.

So, where was she killed?

"And that's not all," Annie added, her tone becoming more serious. "We found a bag of bloody clothes in John Baker's attic. There are also blood stains on the wall in the living room that he tried to wash away, but we found them with the use of luminol. A sample of that blood is in the lab right now, and my guess is it will prove to be Rachel's. As I said, the evidence against him is piling up. He's definitely our guy, but we need to be one hundred percent sure—or as close as we can get, of course. That's where all of you come in. We need to review all the evidence, the crime scene, and everything else with a fine-tooth comb. We can't afford to miss anything. I want us to make absolutely sure we've got everything covered. We need to go through his personal possessions, phone records, and financial transactions to see if anything else can tie him to the crime." Chief Annie paused and looked at all of us. "But personally, I just want to congratulate all of you who work so hard on...."

She didn't get to finish the sentence before someone entered the meeting room. It was the sergeant. He walked up to her and whispered something in her ear. Her eyes grew wide, and she looked at me.

"Okay, listen up, people. I have just been informed that a local patrol was called out very early this morning regarding someone finding something suspicious. They waited for forensics to get there, and it took a while to dig it out. It looks like it's another dead body. And it was found buried in John Baker's backyard."

Chapter 38

"Why are we watching this house?"

David Parker looked at the woman next to him in the car. She was beginning to get on his nerves. Her name was Ivy, she had told him as they drove toward Cocoa Beach, and him jumping into her car when he did was the most exciting thing that had ever happened to her, she claimed. She had been his ticket out of Jacksonville, but now she seemed to want to stick around. Parker let her since being with her made him seem less suspicious. He could send her to get the money he had buried in that small area by I-95 that no one knew about. He could ask her to get them food so no one had to see his face and might recognize him. She was good to have around, especially since the police were looking for a man, not a couple. Plus, she was kind of cute with her blue eyes and brown hair. But boy, she could get on his nerves with all her questions.

"I can't explain why," he said. "I just need to."

She sighed. "We've been watching it for two days now. It's getting dull. I'm bored. This is no fun."

"Well, since this morning, it suddenly got more exciting, don't you think?"

Parker's eyes were fixed on the house at the end of the street. There was a flurry of activity with several police cars and forensic vans parked out front. His heart pounded, and he knew he was taking a huge risk by sitting there, watching.

Parker watched as the police officers went in and out of the house, carrying evidence bags and searching through drawers. His mind raced as he tried to piece together why they were there. What did they find that was so important? What secrets were hidden in this house? He had a feeling he knew. The house had been already blocked off when they got there, but this morning, something had happened, something unusual, and now it was crawling with more police than ever.

Ivy shifted in her seat, obviously uncomfortable with their current situation. "What do you think is going on?" she asked impatiently.

Parker shook his head. "I don't know," he said. "But I think it has something to do with me." He didn't want to tell her why he was watching the house, not yet anyway. He had his suspicions, but he needed more information before he could be certain.

As he watched the house, he couldn't help but feel a pang of fear in his chest. What if they saw him? What if they knew he was here, watching, waiting? He tried to calm himself, telling himself that he was being crazy. But he couldn't shake the feeling that he was being watched, too. He was probably just being paranoid.

"And why do you keep writing things in that notebook of yours?" she asked.

"I'm noting things down so I won't forget," he said. "And I have seen my share of things since we got here. While you were sleeping most of the time."

"Well, I was tired after the long drive. It was quite exhilarating, though," she chirped. "Escaping the long hand of the law. Don't you think?"

He gave her an annoyed look. No, he didn't find any of this exhilarating or even exciting at all. This was his daughter. She had been murdered. He heard on the news when they stopped at a diner that they had found her body—at a freaking storage unit. He had wanted to cry, to shed tears, but the anger that boiled inside him prevented him from doing so. His rage was so intense that he couldn't muster a single tear, only the burning desire to set things right.

Chapter 39

As soon as Matt and I pulled up to the house, we could see the flashing lights of the emergency vehicles. The adrenaline was already coursing through my veins as we approached the front door, where a group of officers was gathered.

"It's in the back," said one of them before leading us through the house and into the backyard, where the body was laid out on a stretcher.

I rushed over to the medical examiner, who was meticulously examining the body. The corpse was caked with dirt and mud, seemingly untouched by human hands since being pulled from the ground. Its eyes were closed, but I imagined them open, wide, and lifeless—just like Rachel's had been. She was naked—just like Rachel had been.

"What do we have here?" I asked, feeling a knot form in my stomach. Was this one another of John Baker's victims? Had he killed before?

"It's a female, approximately thirty-eight years old," she said matter-of-factly. "No identification on her, but she's very obviously been stabbed to death. A single stab wound to the chest."

I let out a frustrated sigh. It sounded just like what had happened to Rachel. This was getting grim. John had a motive for killing Rachel since she wanted to leave him. But why this woman? What was his motive for killing her?

"All right, we need to find out who this Jane Doe is. Can you say if there's a sign of who she might be or who did this?"

The medical examiner shook her head. "Not yet, but we'll run some tests and see what we can come up with. I'll keep you updated."

"Thanks."

I walked over to the stretcher and took a closer look at the woman's face. She was beautiful, with long dark hair and striking green eyes. It was clear that she hadn't been dead for long, and I couldn't help but wonder how long she had been buried out there in the dirt. The dirt looked freshly dug, and the fact that the dog had found it told me it was new, or it would have been found earlier. I shuddered at the thought. I hadn't even considered that John Baker might have killed before. But now, I wondered how many times....

Matt came up beside me, looking pale and shaken. "Do you think it's another one of his victims?" he asked quietly.

"I don't know," I replied. "But we need to find out. I suddenly fear there are more. We need to find out if there are more of them buried out here."

"I'll make sure of that."

I took a deep breath and stepped back, trying to keep my emotions in check. This was no time to panic or let my feelings get the best of me.

"But first, we need to identify this victim. We need to know who she is and her relationship with John Baker."

I turned to the group of officers standing by and gave them a stern look.

"Start canvassing the neighborhood. Ask everyone if they've

seen or heard anything suspicious in the last 24 hours. Ask them if they have seen a woman come here or know who she might be. We need to find out who this woman is and who did this to her," I commanded.

The officers nodded in agreement and quickly dispersed, heading off in different directions to begin their search.

As they left, I turned to Matt and whispered, "This is going to be a long day. Are you ready for this?"

Matt looked at me with a determined expression. "Absolutely. I'll call your mom and have her stay with the children when they come home from school—and pick up Angel from daycare."

"Tell her to make sure Alex brushes his teeth. I found out he hasn't been doing it lately."

Matt smiled vaguely. "Of course."

With that settled, I took a deep breath and headed back to talk to the woman next door whose dog had found the body.

I had a feeling that this case was going to be even more complicated than I had initially thought. John Baker was becoming more and more of a mystery to me, and I didn't know where to start.

Chapter 40

THEN:

Emma's stomach rumbled loudly, breaking the silence between the two girls. They had been walking for hours, and the sun had set long ago. The streets were deserted, and most of the shops had closed. Lily glanced at her sister, her own stomach protesting against the lack of food. The two little girls had no idea where to go or what to do. Their stomachs were rumbling with hunger, and they had no money to buy food.

"I'm hungry," Lily complained and held her stomach.

"I know," Emma said. "Me too."

Lily had tears in her eyes, and they spilled down her cheeks. Emma couldn't stand seeing her like this.

"I need food," she said.

"I don't know where to go," Emma whispered desperately, her voice shaking.

Lily whimpered, her eyes scanning the empty streets for any signs of life. Suddenly, she spotted a small convenience store, its lights still on. She tugged on Emma's sleeve, pointing toward the shop.

"But Lily, I have no money. Do you have any money to buy food?"

"N-no."

Drawn by lights and the thought of food, the girls crept toward the store, their breath held as they stared through the window at all the food. It was all right there—just on the other side of the glass. They could almost reach it. But with no money, they couldn't get it.

Or could they?

Without a word, Emma pushed the door open, and they walked inside. The shelves were stocked with food, and the smell of fresh bread made their mouths water. Lily reached out and grabbed a loaf of bread, and Emma quickly followed suit, grabbing another. They exchanged a quick look, both thinking of the delicious sensation of biting into the bread as soon as they got out of the store.

But as they made their way to the exit, a big man was standing right in front of them. "What do we have here?" he sneered, blocking their path. He reached over and took the bread. "Looks like a couple of little thieves."

"Please, sir, we were just hungry," Emma said, tears in her eyes.

"It's still stealing," he said.

The girls looked at each other, tears welling up in their eyes. They had never stolen anything before, but their hunger had driven them to it. Couldn't he show them mercy?

"I'm sorry," Emma whispered, her voice breaking. "We were just so very hungry."

The store clerk's expression softened slightly, but he still looked stern. "I understand, but that doesn't make it right."

"Please, sir," Emma begged, her eyes brimming with tears. "We won't do it again. Just let us go, and we'll never come back."

The manager stared at them, then shook his head. "You're coming with me."

He grabbed their arms and dragged them, crying and screaming, through the store and into the back room and locked the door.

Chapter 41

My hands shook uncontrollably as I stepped out of the elevator, and my heart pounded. I was so angry I could barely contain it. John Baker had murdered another woman? How many had he killed?

The sound of a hospital monitor beeping echoed off the walls of the hallway. I spotted the doctor at the far end, his face hidden behind a surgical mask. He wasn't alone; a group of nurses surrounded John Baker's bed. As I walked closer, I could feel my anger bubbling up inside me. The only thing I wanted at that moment was for John to wake up so I could get him to admit to what he had done.

"Dr. Calhoun," I said and rushed toward him.

"Agent Thomas," he said.

"Any news on Baker?"

He shook his head sympathetically and said, "I'm afraid not. He's still in a coma."

"Okay, thanks."

The nurses and doctor left. I let out a deep sigh and walked toward John's bed. The monitors beeped steadily, and I leaned in closely, almost whispering to him.

"You're not getting away with what you've done, Baker. You killed two innocent women, one of them my friend, and you're going to pay for it if it's the last thing I do."

I paused, waiting for a response that I knew would never come. I continued, "How many more are there? How many more lives have you destroyed?" But again, there was no response.

Suddenly, I heard a commotion and turned around to see Mrs. Johnson, John's mother-in-law, storming into the room. The guard was trying to stop her, but she pushed through. I guessed they had let her in downstairs because she was immediate family.

I took a deep breath and turned around to face her. She was a formidable woman with a towering presence that seemed to fill the entire room. Her eyes were cold and calculating, her lips set in a thin line of determination. She was clearly not someone to be trifled with. She didn't even look at me as she stormed in and approached the bed.

"Where are they?" she yelled as if she expected John to answer. "Where are the children? What did you do to them, you bastard? You killed my daughter! Murdered her in cold blood, you sick pig. And now we can't find the children! If you have harmed them in any way... I will slit your throat!"

The doctor came in behind her. "Please, keep your voice down, Mrs. Johnson," he said. "This is a hospital."

"Can't you do anything? Can't you wake him up so he can tell me what he has done with the children? Where they are? My lawyer told me that they can come live with me now. I want the children. They're mine now."

"Mrs. Johnson, Madeleine," I said, my voice calm and measured. "I understand that you're upset, but we're doing every-thing we can to find the children."

She snorted derisively. "You're useless. You all are," she said.

"All I care about is my grandchildren. And if you can't find them, then I will."

I shook my head. "I'm sorry, but it doesn't work like that. We have protocols in place to ensure the safety of the children, and we can't just hand them...."

But I didn't get to say anything else. She wasn't listening to me any longer. She just turned around on her heel and walked out of the hospital room.

I shook my head and turned back to John.

"You're not getting away with this," I whispered to him. "I will find those kids. And I'll make sure you pay for all the lives you've ruined. And if you have hurt those children in any way, I swear I will come after you. And you will wish you had died when I shot you. Mark my words."

Chapter 42

Kyla stood in her kitchen, carefully sautéing onions for her homemade pasta sauce. The savory aroma of garlic and Italian spices filled the air. It had been a long day at work, but cooking always helped her unwind. Plus, she had found that it made her forget the sadness of losing her sister for at least a little while.

She was in the middle of stirring the sauce when she heard the sound of a car pulling into her driveway. Kyla glanced out the window and saw her mom's car. She hadn't expected her mom to visit tonight.

As she watched, her mom jumped out of the car and ran toward the front door. Kyla could see the worry etched on her face. Something was wrong.

Before Kyla could even open the door, her mom flung the door open and burst into the house. Kyla rushed to her.

"What's wrong?" she cried, her voice catching in her throat as she took in her mother's strained face. "What's going on?"

Kyla's mom walked past her daughter into the kitchen, her

hand waving in front of her face as she wrinkled her nose. "What is that smell?" she asked, her voice sounding strained and tired.

Kyla's heart sank. "I was just making some pasta sauce."

"Oh, well, in that case, it smells wonderful," she said sarcastically.

"What's going on, Mom?" Kyla asked.

"My lawyer says I can have the kids now that John is going to jail."

"That's good. That's what you wanted, right?" Kyla said.

"Yes," she said with a small snort.

"There's a but coming, isn't there?"

"Yes, dang it. We still don't know where those kids are—what John did with them. Does he have any nearby relatives that he could have taken them to?"

"Not that I know of," she said.

Kyla's mom's voice trailed off as she stared into space, deep in thought. Kyla could see the worry lines on her forehead, and she knew that her mother was trying to come up with a plan.

"We have to find them, Mom," Kyla said, placing a comforting hand on her mother's shoulder.

"I know, honey," her mother said, her voice thick with emotion. "But we don't know where to start."

Kyla shrugged. Her mind raced as she tried to think of a way to help. "Maybe they're with one of his friends? Or co-workers."

"I called the school, and Thomas hasn't been in since Rachel disappeared; the daycare said the same about the twins. No one has seen them since John picked them up after school on the day that Rachel went missing. It worries me."

Kyla's mind was racing, trying to think of any other leads they could follow. "What about social media? Maybe he posted something about where he was taking them?"

Kyla's mom shook her head. "We've been monitoring his

accounts, but there's been nothing. He's gone completely off the grid—even before the coma."

Kyla's heart sank. It seemed like they were at a dead end. Kyla nodded, her mind filled with worry. What if they didn't find them in time? What if John had hurt them? She shook her head as she checked on the pasta sauce. No, she couldn't think like that. John wouldn't harm the children, would he? It seemed unbelievable.

But he did hurt Rachel. He murdered her in cold blood. Don't forget that.

Chapter 43

I was back at the station the next morning, getting ready for our meeting with Chief Annie when the phone rang, and I reached for it automatically, my eyes meeting Matt's across the desk.

"Agent Thomas?" the voice on the other end asked.

"This is she."

"Agent Thomas, this is Dr. Hernandez, the medical examiner you requested to examine the body of the victim buried in the yard."

I leaned forward in my chair, "Yes, Dr. Hernandez. What did you find?"

"I wanted to speak with you in person, Agent Thomas. Can you come down to the morgue?"

I glance at Matt before responding, "Of course, we'll be there in twenty minutes."

I hung up and turned to Matt, "Let's go. We need to speak with the medical examiner in person. The meeting will have to wait."

Matt nodded and stood up, following me out of the station

and into my car. The drive to the morgue was silent, the only sound coming from the car's engine. We were both exhausted from barely any sleep the night before. But getting John Baker for what he had done was a top priority. We'd have to sleep later.

When we arrived, we were greeted by Dr. Hernandez, who led us through the sterile halls to the examination room. The body of the victim was lying on a steel table, covered by a white sheet. Dr. Hernandez stood at the foot of the table, looking solemn.

"Agent Thomas, Detective Miller, thank you for coming," he said as we walked in. "I finished the autopsy, and the results are... disturbing."

I felt a knot form in my stomach as I stepped closer to the table. "What did you find, Doctor?"

Dr. Hernandez removed the sheet that covered the victim's body, revealing the gruesome details of the autopsy. The woman's face was unrecognizable, her features mangled and distorted by what looked like an intense beating. I felt bile rise in my throat as I took in the extent of her injuries.

"She's been assaulted, as you can see," he said and pointed to the marks and bruises. "Beaten."

I closed my eyes, trying to fight off the wave of anger and disgust that washed over me. "Do you have any leads on the suspect? Did you find anything on her?"

Dr. Hernandez shook his head. "The perpetrator wore gloves and a mask, so there's no DNA evidence. The weapon used to inflict the injuries was not found at the scene. She died from a stab wound inflicted after the beating took place. There was one single stab wound to the chest, which was fatal. It happened approximately forty-eight hours ago."

I felt a wave of nausea wash over me at the news. Two days ago. That was pretty recently. A single stab wound to the chest— that was a classic sign of a crime of passion. But who was this woman, and why did Baker murder her too?

I turned to Dr. Hernandez, my mind racing with questions. "Was there anything else? Any signs of struggle or defensive wounds?"

He shook his head solemnly, "No, Agent. It appears to have been a clean, swift attack. There were no signs of defensive wounds or struggle."

I clenched my fists, frustration and anger building inside me. "We could have used something to pin this on Baker. The fact that she was buried in his yard will have to be enough."

Matt placed a hand on my shoulder, offering a small measure of comfort. "We got him already for the murder of Rachel. He's going away for a long time."

I nodded, taking a deep breath to calm myself. "You're right."

I looked at Dr. Hernandez. "Were you able to identify her?"

"As a matter of fact, yes," he said, much to my surprise. I had feared it would take a long time to get this one identified and prepared myself to go over missing person's cases and ask locally if anyone knew her.

"Who is she?" I asked.

"Her name is Elyse Winters."

"Winters?" I asked and looked at Matt. "That was the woman who called Rachel in the middle of the night."

"She was her sister," he added. "She shared twenty-five percent of her DNA with Rachel. That's how I knew they were related—they're half-sisters. I called Mrs. Johnson, and she came down late last night to see her and confirm her identity. She said her daughter, Elyse, had recently moved to Jacksonville, and that's where she thought she was. I'm sure you'll want to talk to her yourself."

My mind raced as I processed the information. This case had just become more complicated than I anticipated. Had John Baker murdered two of Madeline Johnson's daughters? And why Rachel's half-sister?

I turned to Dr. Hernandez, "Thank you, Doctor. We'll need the full autopsy report as soon as possible."

He nodded and handed me a file. "Of course, Agent Thomas. Let me know if you need anything else."

Matt and I left the morgue, both lost in thought. As I started the car, I couldn't help but wonder what other secrets this case held.

When we arrived back at the station, Chief Annie was waiting for us in her office. She looked up as we walked in, her eyes flickering with concern. "Is everything okay?" she asked.

I sighed and took a seat, placing the file on her desk. "We need to talk. We have a new victim... Elyse Winters, another of Madeline's daughters—Rachel Baker's half-sister."

Chief Annie's eyes widened in shock as she took in the information. "Another one? Did John Baker kill them both?"

I nodded, "I don't know. She's been dead for two days. I'm a little wary of how Baker could have done it after I shot him. I thought he was hiding in that abandoned house?"

"So, she was killed later than Rachel? Was it the same MO?"

"Dr. Hernandez just finished the autopsy, and it's clear that she was beaten and then stabbed. Rachel was just stabbed, but other than that, yes, it's the same cause of death, a single stab wound to the chest."

"I wonder how this all pieces together," Chief Annie said. Then, her face lit up. "I guess you can ask Baker that himself. They just called from the hospital while you were out and said he was waking up."

Chapter 44

THEN:

Emma's heart pounded in her chest as the store manager locked her and her sister, Lily, in the small room at the back of the store. The room was barely big enough for the two of them, with nothing but a few boxes stacked in one corner and a small window high up on one wall.

Lily was crying softly, her face buried in Emma's shoulder as Emma tried to soothe her with gentle whispers. Emma knew they had made a mistake by stealing the bread, but they had been so hungry and desperate. They never meant to get caught.

Emma's mind raced with fear and uncertainty as they sat in the darkness. What would happen to them now? Would they be arrested and sent to jail? Would they be separated from each other forever?

Suddenly, the sound of footsteps approached the door, and Emma's heart leaped into her throat. The lock clicked, and the door creaked open, revealing the angry face of the store manager.

"You two are coming with me," he snarled, grabbing Emma's arm and roughly pulling her to her feet.

But as he turned to grab Lily, Emma acted on instinct. She lunged forward and pushed the manager, causing him to stumble back and lose his balance.

It was a split-second decision, but Emma knew it was their only chance at escape. She grasped Lily's hand, and they bolted out of the room and into the store, running as fast as they could toward the front door.

The manager was hot on their heels, shouting and cursing at them, but they were too fast for him. Emma's heart raced as they burst through the door and onto the street, the warm night air hitting their faces.

Heart pounding, Emma looked around frantically for a place to hide. She spotted an alleyway nearby and grabbed Lily's hand, pulling her toward it. They darted into the shadows and crouched behind a pile of trash cans. That's when they saw the police car darting by and stopping by the store. Emma stared at the police officers getting out, gasping. It had been so close—too close.

Lily looked up at Emma with grateful tears in her eyes. "Thank you," she whispered.

Emma nodded, still catching her breath. "We have to keep moving," she said. "We can't stay here."

Together, they got up and began walking down the alley, trying to blend in. They had no idea where they were going or what they were going to do next, but they knew they couldn't go back to their old life.

They didn't stop walking until they were several blocks away, their legs aching. Finally, they slowed down and caught their breath, looking at each other with a mix of relief and fear.

"What do we do now?" Lily asked, her voice trembling.

Emma took a deep breath and looked around at the dark, empty streets. They were alone and had nowhere to go, but she couldn't let Lily see her fear.

"We keep running," she said, taking Lily's hand once again. "We'll figure it out together."

Emma and Lily walked cautiously along the deserted street, keeping an eye out for any signs of danger. They had been walking for hours, and exhaustion was beginning to set in. Emma's stomach growled with hunger, but she knew they couldn't risk stealing anything else.

Just as they were about to turn a corner, a police officer suddenly appeared in front of them, blocking their path. He had a stern look on his face as he approached them, his hand resting on his gun.

"Stop right there," he commanded, his voice booming through the quiet street. "What are you two doing out here at this hour?"

Emma felt her heart sink as she realized they had been caught again. She didn't know how much longer they could keep running.

"We were just walking," she said, trying to keep her voice steady. "We don't mean any harm."

The officer looked at them suspiciously, his eyes scanning their faces for any signs of guilt. "Where do you live?"

"N-nowhere, or rather no, we live down that street," she said, hoping he wouldn't realize they had nowhere to go and that she was lying to him.

He glared down at them, his look stern. "I think I need to take you to the station. Come with me."

Chapter 45

Matt and I rushed through the hospital's automatic doors, our badges held over our heads like a white flag. The security guard recognized us both immediately, his eyes full of understanding for what we were about to face. He simply nodded before allowing us access, and we continued on without another word.

We hurried down the white-tiled hallway, our shoes slapping loudly on the floor. A few nurses hurried past us with anxious glances, and a doctor stood at the end of the hall, frantically typing on a tablet.

As we approached John's room, we could hear the steady beeping of the machines monitoring his vital signs. Dr. Calhoun, the top surgeon at the hospital, the man who had removed the bullet I put in John, was already there, examining John with a look of grave concern on his face.

"Detectives," he greeted us, not looking up from his patient. "I take it you got my message?"

He turned to look at us with a smile.

"Yes," I said. "He's awake?"

"He's waking up slowly," Dr. Calhoun said, feeling Baker's pulse on his wrist. "It will take a little time before he is fully himself."

"But can we talk to him?" Matt asked.

The doctor looked at his patient and then back at us. "He's still quite groggy, but he should be able to answer a few questions. But make it brief, please. He needs rest."

Matt and I exchanged a look before we stepped closer to John's bed. He looked smaller somehow, more fragile than I remembered. His face was pale, his eyes closed, and his chest rose and fell with the steady beep of the machines.

"John," I said, "It's Agent Thomas. Can you hear me?"

There was a moment of silence before he stirred, his eyelids fluttering open. He looked up at me with a dazed expression, his eyes struggling to focus.

"Thomas?" he murmured, his voice rough and weak. "Who is Thomas?"

I exchanged a glance with Matt, who shook his head slightly, indicating that I should continue to talk to John. I leaned closer to him, trying to keep my voice soft and reassuring.

"John, it's me, Agent Thomas. Do you remember what happened to you?" I asked.

John groaned softly, his eyes closing again for a moment before he opened them once more.

"The shooting," he muttered. "I remember the shooting. There was pain. A lot of pain, and it went on for a very long time."

"Good," Matt said, relief washing over his face. "He does remember."

"You were fleeing from the police," I said.

John's brows furrowed in concentration, and he struggled to speak. "I... I don't remember," he said after a moment. "It... it all happened so fast."

Matt stepped forward, his expression serious. "John, we need you to try and remember."

"I am trying, dang it," he said and winced in pain.

"Where are the children?" I asked.

He gave me a look, eyes narrow, a frown between his brows. "What children?"

"He's playing us," Matt said. "Don't buy into it."

Matt approached John. "Your children... Thomas and the twins. You hid them somewhere so their grandmother couldn't see them. We need to know that they're okay—that you didn't hurt them."

John's face contorted with confusion and pain. "I... I don't have any children," he said, his voice almost a whisper. "What are you talking about?"

Matt and I exchanged a look of disbelief. How could he not remember his own children? Unless he was lying to us.

"John, you had the children," I said sternly. "You were hiding them from their grandmother. We need you to tell us where they are and whether they're safe."

John's eyes widened in fear, and he tried to sit up, but Dr. Calhoun gently pushed him back down. "You need to rest, John," he said. "Your injuries are serious."

But John was frantic now, his eyes darting around the room. "I don't have any children!" he exclaimed. "I don't know what you're talking about!"

"Please, don't anger my patient," the doctor said. "He's in no condition to be agitated right now. You'll have to come back and ask him questions later."

"I swear, I don't remember," John added. "I don't recall any of this."

"Not even your wife?" Matt asked. "Who went missing and was found dead in your storage unit? The one you had rented?"

John looked at us, perplexed. "What? Rachel is dead?"

"Oh, so you do remember your wife," Matt said.

"Yes, of course, I remember her. We were just married a few months ago."

"It would appear that the patient is suffering from some sort of memory loss," Dr. Calhoun said. "I think we need to evaluate him to determine how severe this is. I will have to ask you to leave for now. His health is more important, to me at least."

Matt and I exchanged another look. This wasn't going anywhere. We needed to find another way to get the information. I motioned for Matt to follow me out of the room before turning to Dr. Calhoun.

"Doctor, do you know if John had any visitors during his stay here?" I asked.

He thought for a moment before nodding. "There was a woman who came to see him yesterday. She asked about him downstairs but was told that she couldn't see him since he was in the ICU and in police custody. Only immediate family was allowed in. I was there to talk to a patient's relatives when I heard her ask for him. She left without leaving her name, but I remember overhearing the conversation."

"Can you describe her to us?" Matt asked.

Dr. Calhoun furrowed his brows, trying to recall the woman's features. "She had long black hair and big brown eyes. She was wearing a red top and small jeans shorts."

"Matt and I need to find this woman," I said. "Can you give us the security footage from the day she visited?"

"Of course. If you'll just come with me, I'll show you to our security room."

Chapter 46

Kyla and her mom tiptoed down the hospital corridor, glancing left and right for any sign of a guard or nurse. They had used Rachel's card to get in through the back way. Since she was a nurse practitioner, she had access to areas most people didn't. Her mom said she had taken it from Rachel's belongings at the house.

The hallway's darkness was broken up by harsh fluorescent lighting, casting a bluish-green hue onto the walls. Kyla's mother marched forward with purpose while Kyla tried to keep up, her stomach churning with trepidation. She knew what her mother had in mind—run into John's room, confront him about what he did to Rachel, and make him tell where he hid the children. They had heard he was awake and able to talk.

Kyla thought it was an awful idea. She wanted to grab her mom's arm and yank her back, but the determined look on her mom's face made it clear that there would be no stopping her this time. As the police officer sitting outside the room left to get coffee, they snuck past him.

The room was illuminated only by the faint flickering of a

nightlight, and John lay in his bed as still as a statue. Suddenly, his eyes fluttered open, and he blinked several times, trying to adjust to the dim light. Kyla's mom stalked forward like an angry lioness, her gaze sharp enough to cut through the darkness.

"Madeleine? W-what are you doing here?" he asked.

Kyla's mom yelled. "You killed my daughter, you monster!"

John's eyes shot wide open, and he looked around the room confusedly. His eyes met Kyla's, and she could tell he had no idea what was happening. "I don't understand," he said weakly. "I don't remember anything."

His reaction took Kyla aback. She had expected him to be defensive or even hostile; it was strange to her. But her mother didn't step down. His not admitting to having done it only fueled her anger toward him.

"How can you not remember? You murdered her, you bastard!"

John Baker's eyes widened in shock. "I don't remember that," he protested weakly. "I don't remember anything."

Kyla's mom refused to back down. She was on a roll now. "Don't lie to me," she hissed. "You know exactly what I'm talking about. She was going to leave you, and you stabbed her. They found blood in your house, the one you shared with Rachel, where you built a family. She gave you children. You didn't deserve her; you never did. You killed her."

"I'm sorry," John said, his voice barely above a whisper. "I don't remember anything before I was shot. The police told me stuff, but I swear, I don't remember anything."

"Liar," she hissed.

Kyla walked closer and grabbed her mother's shoulder. "Maybe we should...."

Her mom pulled out of her grip. "No, we shouldn't. I'm not done with him yet. I want the children. Where have you hidden them?"

"I swear," John said, almost in tears. "I don't recall anything. I don't know what you're talking about. What children? Rachel and I just got married!"

The tension in the room was palpable as Kyla's mom stood there, her eyes narrowed and her fists clenched. Kyla watched, her heart heavy with grief and anger. She wondered if John was telling the truth or if he was just pretending not to remember.

"You sick bastard," her mother spat. "Don't you lie to me."

Then she lunged at him. Seeing this, Kyla sprang forward to grab her mother. She had her hands wrapped around his throat and was pressing hard. Kyla tried to pull her away from him, but she was freakishly strong for such a small woman.

Suddenly, the door burst open, and a doctor rushed in, followed closely by the police officer who had been guarding the door. The doctor took one look at Kyla's mom, then yelled:

"What's going on in here? You need to leave at once," he said sternly, eyeing Kyla and her mother suspiciously.

The officer came up behind him and gave them a look to make them understand the severity of the situation.

Kyla's mom turned to the doctor, her face red with anger, her eyes still blazing. "This is not over," she yelled as they left the room. "This is far from over," she repeated before storming down the hallway with Kyla in tow.

Kyla followed her mother out of the hospital, feeling a strange mix of emotions. She was angry at John for what she believed he had done to her sister, but she was also confused by his apparent lack of memory. She had so many questions and didn't know where to start looking for answers.

As they made their way to their car and got in, Kyla's mom continued to fume. "He's lying," she muttered. "I know he is. We need to find out the truth and make him pay for what he did. I know exactly how we're going to do it."

Chapter 47

I sat at the computer in the dimly lit room of the police station, my eyes fixed on the screen in front of me. The small glowing monitor illuminated my face as I scrolled through the footage. Matt stood beside me, his arms folded across his chest as we watched the surveillance footage from the hospital lobby.

We had been at the police station for hours now, sifting through endless hours of surveillance footage from the hospital. The sound of the computer fan whirred in the silence, the only noise in the room. I could feel my eyelids getting heavy as the surveillance tapes cycled through, searching for that one person we thought held the answers.

Suddenly, my eyes caught something in the footage. A woman had just walked up to the front desk in the hospital lobby and talked to the lady behind the counter. At first, we couldn't hear what they were saying, but as she snapped tersely, talking soon became yelling, so it could be heard loud and clear on the footage.

"I need to see him; I need to see Mr. Baker. Let me through—it's an emergency!"

The lady behind the desk crossed her arms and replied

stoically, "I'm sorry, ma'am, no visitors are allowed. He is in police custody."

The woman then began to plead with the receptionist, her voice urgent and desperate as she waved her hands in frustration. Her eyes darted around the room furtively. But she wasn't let through. Then, a security guard approached her, and she calmed down. She was told to leave.

We watched as the woman finished her conversation and walked away. I studied the footage closely just as she turned to look back at the desk with a look of sorrowful desperation. Just before she disappeared from view, we paused the footage and zoomed in on her face.

"There," I said, pointing to the frozen image of her face. "That's her. That's the woman Dr. Calhoun talked about."

I studied her face, etching it into my memory, haunting me with its familiarity. Where had I seen her before? I gasped as recognition hit me like a ton of bricks.

"I know who she is," I said, my voice shrill with surprise. "I know exactly who that woman is. That's Emily Matthew—the mother of Christopher Matthew from Alex's grade. What on earth is she doing there? Why is she trying to visit John Baker?"

Matt spun around to me, eyes wide and mouth agape. "You're right," he whispered, his voice heavy with disbelief. He leaned in for a better view, slowly nodding in agreement. His face darkened as he murmured, "Yeah, that's definitely her. I remember seeing her when dropping off the kids—and that time we had a multi-cultural night at the school, and she brought in those soggy nachos."

I couldn't shake off the feeling that there was more to the story than just a concerned mother trying to visit a patient in the hospital or a fellow parent she knew from school. Emily Matthew had always been a strange woman, but this was a whole new level of odd behavior. I turned to Matt, my mind racing with possibilities.

"We need to talk to her," I said firmly. "We need to find out what she was doing there and what connection she has to John Baker."

Matt nodded in agreement, and we quickly gathered our things, ready to leave for Emily's house.

As we drove down A1A, I couldn't help but feel a sense of unease settle in the pit of my stomach. Something about the whole situation just didn't feel right.

Chapter 48

Parker nursed his drink at the Beach Shack while Ivy cheerfully regaled him with stories. It was a small, shady place where he didn't fear anyone would recognize him, and even if they did, they wouldn't care enough to call the cops on him.

They had been living in the car for days now, and he needed to get out. He had been keeping an eye on John Baker's house and knew they had found another body there. He had watched from a distance as they went through the house, combing it for evidence. But he didn't know where John Baker was. Anger boiled inside him when he thought of what had been done to his daughter. Parker wasn't close to Rachel by any means, but that wasn't his fault. He had tried all through her upbringing to be there, to have a relationship with her, sending her endless letters from prison but without success. And now she was gone. It broke his heart.

Ivy's high-pitched voice filled the small room, and he couldn't make out what she was saying as her words blended together into a single rushed stream. He nodded along, half-listening until something on the TV mounted on the wall caught his eye—it was tuned to the local news channel.

"What's this about?" he murmured, leaning forward slightly and squinting to make out the headlines scrolling across the bottom of the screen.

Ivy's voice was a constant chatter, and her words seemed to echo in his ears each time she spoke. It felt like he was trying to listen through a thick fog and struggled to make out what she was saying.

"Can you please be quiet for a second?" Parker interrupted Ivy.

She stopped mid-sentence, looking at him quizzically. He gestured toward the TV, where the volume had been turned down low. Parker motioned to the bartender, signaling for him to turn up the sound.

The reporter's voice filled the bar, talking about a suspect who had been apprehended in connection with the murder of Rachel Baker. Parker's heart rate quickened as he listened to the details. The suspect had been in a coma for a few days but was now waking up.

John Baker.

Parker slammed back the rest of his beer, tossed a few bills on the bar, and made a beeline for the door. Ivy followed him outside, her heels clicking loudly on the pavement.

"What's going on, Parker?" she asked as he fished the car keys out of his pocket.

"John Baker's been caught," he said, his voice low and tense with barely contained rage. "And I'm going to pay him a little visit."

Ivy looked at him with a mix of concern and fear. "Parker, please don't do anything stupid. You'll just end up back in jail or worse."

Parker didn't respond; he just got into the car's driver's seat and started the engine. Ivy jumped in the passenger's seat, barely making it inside before he took off. Her eyes were fixed on Parker as he sped away from the Beach Shack.

As they drove toward the hospital where John Baker was being treated, Parker's mind was consumed with thoughts of revenge. He knew that he shouldn't take matters into his own hands—that it was foolish and dangerous. But Rachel had been taken from him just as she had come back into his life. There was no way he could just watch while this murderer got away with it. Having been in jail for years, he knew it was far from punishment enough.

Chapter 49

Emily Matthews opened the door, her eyes widening in surprise as she took in Matt and me on her doorstep. Her lips were pursed slightly, and one hand was gripping the edge of the door handle tightly, the other reaching up to touch her forehead where a furrow of worry had formed.

"Eva Rae? Matt? What's going on? Is something wrong with Alex?" she asked. "Has something happened? Did he and Christopher get into another fight at school?"

I could feel Emily's eyes on me as I replied, my voice calm but not quite reassuring. "No, it's not about Alex," I said. "We're here on police business. Can we come in?"

The confusion that crossed her face was clear—her lips parted slightly, and her eyebrows furrowed. Her whole body seemed to shake as she asked, "Police business? What's going on?"

"Let's talk inside, shall we?" I said.

Emily stood still for a few seconds, her eyes wide and her brow furrowed. She slowly grabbed her purse off a nearby table and held it tight against her chest. Her gaze darted between me and the door as if calculating her escape route. She opened her mouth to say something but hesitated, pressing her lips together in an awkward silence before finally muttering, "I was just leaving."

As I watched her move toward me, blocking the doorway with my body, I couldn't help but wonder what had brought on this sudden change of heart.

Just then, I heard a chorus of giggles emanating from behind her. It sounded like two or three little voices—definitely more than the three-year-old I knew she had or nine-year-old Christopher's.

"Are you having playdates over?" I asked. "And are you about to leave while they're here?"

I knew she was a single mom, and the dad had left last year and had not talked to her or the children since. She had no parents living here who could help her babysit. Was she about to leave them alone in the house?

I elbowed past Emily Matthews before she could say anything, and her face drained of color. As I rushed by, I couldn't help but notice the deep furrow in her brow and the fear that welled up behind her eyes. My chest tightened as my sneakers thudded against the floorboards of her hallway, echoing through the entire house. Matt and I stepped into a wide living room, my pulse pounding like thunder in my ears.

As I entered the room, my eyes fell upon two little ones whom I instantly recognized. Robert and Maria Baker, Rachel's twin children, were arguing over a pile of blocks. The sight of them brought a lump to my throat. They looked so much like their mother, and before I knew it, tears threatened to spill from my lashes. Thomas, Alex's pal and Rachel's older son, sat on the sofa with an intense look on his face as he played a video game. Emily stood beside me; her shoulders sagged in resignation as she let out a breath.

"I think we need to talk," I said.

Her face blanched even more, and she swallowed hard, putting the purse back on the table.

"Of course, anything I can do to help," she said, her voice trembling. "Let's sit in the kitchen."

Chapter 50

THEN:

Emma and Lily sat in the cold metal chairs of the police station, their bodies trembling with fear. Emma held Lily close, her arms wrapped tightly around her sister's waist, trying to reassure her as they waited to know their fate. Would they send them back to their mother? Would they go to jail for stealing the bread?

Lily was sobbing, her thin frame shaking with each ragged breath she took. Emma wrapped her arm around Lily's shoulder, pulling her close.

"Shh, it's going to be okay," she whispered, even though she wasn't sure if it was the truth.

Lily's eyes were red and swollen from crying, her breath coming in short gasps as she attempted to calm herself. Emma held her hand, rubbing her thumb over the back of it in a soothing gesture.

The room was a chaotic rush of people coming in and out, and it frightened Emma. Emma could feel the weight of the situation pressing down on her, the fear of what might come next, causing her heart to race.

The sound of footsteps echoed down the hallway, causing the girls to jump. A tall, imposing figure appeared in the doorway, his stern expression softening slightly when he saw the two young girls huddled together.

"Emma and Lily?" he asked, his voice low and gravely.

The girls nodded, their hearts racing.

"Y-yes?"

He sat down next to them, folding his hands. "I'm afraid I have some bad news."

Emma looked at him, eyes growing wide. "W-what news?"

"It's your mother," he said with an exhale. "She tried to kill herself. She's in the hospital still."

The news hit Emma and Lily like a ton of bricks. They both knew it was their fault because they had run away. Emma felt a massive wave of guilt wash over her. Maybe if she had been a better daughter, their mother wouldn't have felt so alone. If only they had never run away.

If only.

Lily's sobs turned into quiet whimpers as the reality of the situation set in. Emma held her tighter, unsure of what to say or do to make things better.

The police officer cleared his throat, breaking the heavy silence. "You girls won't be charged with stealing the bread, but we'll need to sort out temporary custody until your mother is better."

Emma nodded, feeling a glimmer of relief. At least they wouldn't be sent to jail.

The officer stood up, his shadow stretching across the room. "I'll give you some time to process everything," he said before leaving the room.

Emma and Lily sat in silence for a few moments, the weight of their mother's situation heavy on their hearts. Emma wanted to say something, to make things better, but the words caught in her throat.

Finally, Lily spoke up, her voice heavy with grief. "Do you think she'll be okay?"

Emma took a deep breath, hoping to find the right words. "I don't know, but we'll be there for her. We'll be strong for her."

Lily nodded, wiping away her tears. "Okay," she said, her voice still shaky.

Emma leaned in, kissing the top of Lily's head. "We'll get through this together," she promised.

As the minutes ticked by, the girls sat in a haze of emotions, their minds racing with worry and uncertainty. They both knew they would be able to weather this storm, too. All they had to do was be better—be perfect.

Chapter 51

I had entered Emily Matthew's house with Matt and looked around the kitchen, taking in the comfortable furniture and the cozy ambiance. Emily, a tall, slender woman with auburn hair, was pouring iced tea for us, and I couldn't help but notice how her hands trembled slightly. Matt and I sat on the chairs, and Emily finally sat across from us, sipping her tea. Emily fidgeted in her seat, her eyes staring at the floor as if looking for the right answer. I could hear the children playing in the living room.

"So, tell me, Emily," I said, "Why did John leave the children here with you?"

Emily looked down at her tea, her face flushing slightly. She took a deep breath, her eyes still glued to the ground. "John and I have been seeing each other," she said quietly.

Matt and I exchanged a look of surprise.

"What do you mean, seeing each other?" Matt asked.

Emily shifted in her seat, still avoiding eye contact. "We've been having an affair," she said. "It sounds so bad when you say it out loud. But we really care about one another. He told me he was going to leave her eventually."

I could feel my heart rate increase as Matt and I looked at each other in disbelief. "How long has this been going on?" I asked.

Emily shrugged. "A few months," she said. "He's been having problems with his wife, and we just sort of... fell into it."

"And why are the children here with you?" I asked.

"He's hiding them from his mother-in-law. She wants to take the children away from him. That's what he said. When Rachel went missing, he feared they'd be taken away from him."

Matt furrowed his eyebrows. "His mother-in-law?" he repeated, "Why would he need to hide the children from her?"

Emily sighed heavily. "John's mother-in-law is a very controlling woman," she explained. "She wanted the kids. At least that's what he said to me. She's been saying he's not fit to raise them. He didn't want them to be taken away, so he asked me to look after them until things calmed down. I have to admit I was skeptical at first. Not to take in the kids, but the whole Rachel going missing thing. I worried...," she paused and looked at her hands. "I worried that he had hurt her, you know? To get rid of her. It's been bothering me. I needed to know the truth."

"Was that why you came to the hospital? To talk to him?" I asked.

"Partly that, but also to see if he was okay. I had heard that he had been shot, and I was concerned. I guess I still love him. But then I heard on the news that he was considered a suspect, and that scared me, you know? I wanted... no, I needed some answers from him. I still do."

"Do you believe he could be capable of hurting Rachel? Of killing her?" I asked.

She hesitated before answering. "I... I do. He's mentioned before that he wanted to get rid of her. Those were his words. I've been lying awake every night since she went missing, thinking about it and whether to tell the police. I can't believe she's dead. But I also care for him, you know? I didn't want him to get in any sort of trouble. And when it first started out, and Rachel was gone, I told him I could tell them—you—about where he was that morning when she went missing. But he didn't want me to."

"You can provide an alibi for him?" I asked with a frown.

She nodded. "Absolutely. He dropped off the kids at daycare with Rachel. I was there too, dropping off my youngest, then Rachel drove him to his work downtown, where she dropped him off, and then instead of going inside the building where his office is, he met me down on the beach. We went for a walk, trying to talk because we hadn't been able to see one another all weekend. We usually met on the beach or sometimes in his car to go for a ride. Sometimes, he took me to his storage space, and we had... sex in the car there. I'm not proud of it, but it is what it is. And I'm not proud to say this either, but he usually pays me for it."

I sighed. This wasn't pretty. It made me feel awful for Rachel. Had she known? Did she find this out? And that's why he killed her?

"But just to be certain I heard you correctly... John didn't want you to tell us that he was with you on that morning his wife disappeared, even though it gave him an alibi?" I asked, puzzled.

"He was afraid Rachel would find out that we were having an affair. So, I guess he couldn't have known that she was dead, huh?"

I had to admit that she made a valid point. Why would John refuse to get his alibi out if he knew Rachel was dead? Why would he still try to protect her feelings? To not risk losing the children? But he would anyway if he was convicted and going to jail.

It didn't really add up.

As I pondered this, Matt spoke up, "Emily, you have to understand that we are trying to get to the bottom of this case. If you know anything that can help us, you need to tell us. Otherwise, you could be interfering with justice," he said sternly.

Emily nodded, her eyes filling with tears. "I know," she whispered. "This is all I know. I want to help. I really do. I just... I didn't want to believe it was possible. But now, I'm scared, too. I don't know what to do."

I got up from the chair and walked to the living room and looked at the children. "We're taking them with us for now," I said. "A judge has awarded temporary custody of them to their grandmother."

"O-okay," she said with a sniffle. "Let me get their things together. Then you can take them."

Chapter 52

John Baker lay in his hospital bed, staring up at the sterile ceiling tiles. He couldn't sleep—the pain medication had left him feeling restless. His body was aching, and his mind was racing. It was the middle of the night, and he couldn't seem to shake the feeling that something was wrong. He turned his head to look out the window, but all he could see was the reflection of the dimly lit hospital room. He shifted in the bed, trying to get comfortable, when he heard a faint rustling sound. He turned his head, looking toward the door, but it was closed, and he couldn't see anyone.

"Hello?" he called out, his voice hoarse and weak. "Who's there?"

There was no response, and John started to feel foolish. He was probably just being paranoid, he told himself. After all, he was in a hospital with plenty of security. There was no way anyone could get to him.

He closed his eyes and tried to relax, but the fear remained. He couldn't shake the feeling that something was off. The painkillers they had given him were making him feel drowsy, but his mind was racing with thoughts of what would happen next. Would he ever fully recover? Would he be able to work? Would he even be able to remember again? He felt so confused. The police seemed to think he had murdered Rachel, but why couldn't he remember anything? It was like the past ten years were gone, evaporated from his mind. They told him they had children, but he didn't remember them. And now they said that Rachel was gone? His beloved wife that he just married was dead?

And I killed her?

As he lay there, he suddenly heard a sound that made him sit up in bed. Someone was in the room with him. He couldn't see anyone, but he could feel a presence.

"Who's there?" he called out, his voice hoarse from the breathing tube.

There was no answer. He felt a prickling sense of fear creeping up his spine. Maybe it was just his imagination, but he couldn't shake the feeling that someone was watching him.

John felt a chill run down his spine. He was scared and confused. Was it a nurse? A doctor?

He told himself he was being paranoid, that he was safe in the hospital, but he couldn't shake the feeling. He tried to calm himself, closing his eyes and taking deep breaths.

Then he felt something soft and heavy pressing down on his face—a pillow. He struggled, trying to pull it away, but he was too weak. The figure behind the pillow was strong, and he couldn't break free. His vision started to fade as he gasped for air. He could feel his body slipping away, his thoughts becoming muddled. He didn't want to die like this, alone and scared. He tried to call out, to scream for help, but no sound would come out.

He couldn't breathe. Panic set in as he realized someone was trying to suffocate him. He thrashed around as much as he could, but his body was weighed down. The room spun around him as he fought for air, but he knew he was losing the battle. His vision started to darken around the edges, and his body grew still as he lost consciousness.

Chapter 53

We went home and had dinner with the kids. Angel was throwing food as usual, and Alex didn't eat much. He told us he was worried about Thomas. I told him he was safe with his grandmother now, as I had taken him and the twins there myself. Madeleine Johnson had been so grateful to get them home, as she put it. And their cousin Charlie was there too, so they weren't the only children in the house.

Madeleine hugged me and told me thank you so many times that it became almost embarrassing. I was just happy they were safe and that they could now return to school and friends and have as normal a life as possible, even though it looked like they had lost their mom and dad all at once.

Once my kids left the table, Matt and I sat in the living room, bringing my glass of wine and talking about the case. He sipped his beer while I nursed my glass of Chardonnay.

"John Baker has an alibi," I said thoughtfully. "We need to seriously take that into consideration, along with the fact that Elyse Winters was killed after I shot him. How would he have been able to drive all the way to Jacksonville, kill her, bring her back, and bury her in his yard with a gunshot wound in his shoulder? He might not be our guy after all."

Matt nodded. "You're making a valid point, but I'm still not convinced. Yes, he has an alibi, but from whom? Think about it."

"I know she's his lover," I said. "But it's still an alibi."

Matt furrowed his brow. "Not a very strong one. She could be lying because she cares about him."

I shook my head. "She didn't seem like she cared about him much when we talked to her." I took another sip of my wine. "It's hard to tell."

We sat in silence for a moment. The clock on the wall ticked away the minutes, but there was no answer in the ticking.

Matt swirled his beer bottle before taking a long sip and setting it down on the table.

"Maybe she's covering for him. Or maybe she's scared of him," he said thoughtfully.

I took a sip of my wine, contemplating his words. "That's possible. But we need more evidence before we can come to any conclusions."

As if she had heard me, the chief suddenly called, and I picked up.

"Chief Annie? What's up?" I asked.

"I'm sorry to disturb you so late, but I was still at the station and thought you would want to know this."

I sat up straight on my couch. "Know what?"

"The lab results came in tonight, and I'm just now seeing them. This is not good for our case against John Baker."

"What's going on? What do they show?"

She cleared her throat. "The blood in his house, on the wall... it wasn't Rachel's."

"Could it be her sister's? Elyse Winter's? The one we found in the backyard?" I asked.

"Not hers either. Get this... it was John's own blood. This backs up his testimony before he was shot that he had an accident and a nosebleed."

"Dang it," I said. "I was so sure it would be Rachel's."

"There's more."

"Now what?"

"The clothes, the ones that were found in a plastic bag in the attic of his house... the blood on them was, in fact, a match with Rachel's, but...."

"But what?"

"There's no DNA from John on them. If he had put them in the bag and hid them, there would most likely be his DNA as well if he had touched them or from sweat and oils. They were Rachel's clothes she was wearing when she was killed, but her body was naked when found. The only DNA trail of John's found inside the garbage bag with the clothes was from a pizza crust that was somehow in there too—in the pants pocket."

"A pizza crust?" I asked. "That's an odd thing to find among hidden bloody clothes from a murder?"

"It sure is. But it had John Baker's DNA all over it."

I hung up and looked at Matt, who had been listening in on our conversation.

"This just got more complicated," I said, setting down my wine glass. "John's alibi might be stronger than we thought."

Matt nodded. "But there's still something fishy going on. Why would there be a pizza crust with his DNA in the same bag as Rachel's bloody clothes?"

"I don't know," I said, rubbing my temples. "But we need to find out. And we need to talk to John again."

Matt stood up, grabbing his coat. "Let's go. We can't waste any time."

I gripped the steering wheel tightly as I raced down A1A, accelerating through the yellow lights. Inside the car, a thousand questions whirled through my mind, and I had trouble focusing on where I was going. John was in there recovering from a gunshot wound that I had inflicted upon him, and I felt my stomach twist in knots at the thought that if he didn't regain his memory, that was what would keep us from getting to the truth.

Chapter 54

Matt and I rushed into the hospital, our hearts pounding as we made our way to the front desk. The lady behind the counter looked up at us and raised her eyebrows, but we wasted no time in showing her our badges.

"We're here to see John Baker," Matt said, his voice urgent.

The woman nodded and handed us visitor badges before pointing us toward the elevators. We stepped inside and hit the button for the third floor, our minds racing with thoughts of what we might find when we reached John's room.

As the elevator doors slid open, we could see an officer slumped against the wall, his head hanging low. Panic coursed through my veins as I realized that something was wrong.

"Hey, wake up!" I shouted, shaking the officer's shoulder.

He groaned and lifted his head, his eyes bleary and unfocused.

"What on earth is going on here?" I demanded, my voice rising. "You were supposed to be protecting the door."

The officer mumbled something incoherent, then sat up straight.

"I'm sorry... I must have dozed off for a few seconds."

I stared at him, my emotions roiling inside me. Matt stepped forward, his hand on my shoulder as if to steady me.

"We need to check on John," he said, his voice low and urgent.

We made our way to John's room, and I felt my stomach churn as I saw that the door was ajar. Without hesitation, I pushed it open and rushed inside. The scene that greeted me was one of absolute horror.

John lay there, lifeless, his eyes staring blankly at the ceiling, his skin pale. The monitors were beeping and blinking rapidly. Matt rushed in behind me, his eyes widening in horror at the sight before us.

"Oh, my God," he whispered, his voice barely audible.

I felt a scream building inside me, but it got caught in my throat, leaving me gasping for air.

Matt moved past me, his eyes scanning the room for any signs of what might have happened. I watched as he checked John's pulse, then turned to me, his expression grim. I felt a lump form in my throat as I stared down at John's body. How did this happen? How had no one heard the monitors go off? It had to have happened very recently, as just now the nurses came rushing. Was the killer still here?

"He's gone," he said, his voice flat. "We need to call this in." Matt pulled out his phone and made the call while I stood there, numb and in shock. I told them to close down the hospital in case the killer was still here.

As we waited for backup to arrive, my mind raced with thoughts of who could have done this. The pillow was on the ground next to him, and I had no doubt in my mind that it was what the killer used. I felt a wave of guilt wash over me as I thought about how John had been under our protection and we had failed him. Who could have done this to him? Was it someone we knew?

Was it the same person who killed Rachel and Elyse? It all felt so confusing to me.

When backup finally arrived, they took over the scene, and we were instructed to leave. Matt and I stepped out into the hallway, our faces grim and our hearts heavy.

"I can't believe this happened," I said, my voice still shivering. "We were supposed to protect him."

Matt put a hand on my shoulder, his touch comforting. He nodded, his jaw set in determination. "We'll find out who did this, and we'll make sure they pay. That's a promise."

Chapter 55

Kyla paced back and forth in her bedroom, frantically throwing clothes into her suitcase. She had to leave; she had to get out of town.

And fast.

As she moved, the TV in the background droned on with the news report she'd been watching for the past hour. It blared from the television mounted on the wall, the anchor's voice ringing through the room.

"...The man was found dead in his hospital bed, smothered to death with what appears to be a pillow. Police have yet to identify a suspect, but they are urging anyone with information to come forward."

Kyla froze, staring at the TV screen. She just stood there, paralyzed, her hands shaking as she watched the footage of the hospital's entrance. Kyla's hands were still trembling as she zipped up her suitcase, her mind racing with thoughts of what might happen next.

You need to get out of here. Now.

Her phone rang, jolting her out of her panicked thoughts. It was her mother.

"What are you doing?" her mother asked.

"N-nothing."

"You were supposed to come over tonight, weren't you?" she asked, her tone angry.

"Y-yes. But something came up."

"Really? And what was that something? What could be more important than being with your mother and your dead sisters' children?"

It was the way she said it that bothered her—dead sisters—like she blamed her for both of their deaths.

Kyla took a deep breath and tried to keep her composure. "I'm sorry, Mom. I'll make it up to you and the kids."

There was a long pause on the other end of the line. Kyla could hear her mother's heavy breathing.

"You know, Kyla," her mother finally said. "You're always running away from your problems. You can't keep doing that forever."

Kyla felt a sudden surge of frustration. "I'm not running away from anything, Mom!" she snapped. "I just need some time to figure things out."

Her mother sighed. Kyla took a deep breath, trying to calm her racing heart. "I'm sorry, Mom. I can't make it tonight. I'll come over soon; I promise."

Her mother sighed. "Fine. But you have to make it up to us. We're still grieving, and we need you here."

"I know," Kyla said softly, feeling a pang of guilt in her chest. Both of her sisters' deaths had hit them all hard, but Kyla was the only one who had to deal with the aftermath alone. She couldn't stay here, not with the police closing in.

"I have to go, Mom. I love you," she said hurriedly before hanging up.

She grabbed her suitcase and headed for the door, feeling a sense of urgency wash over her. She had no plan, no destination, but she knew she couldn't stay here any longer.

As she walked out the door, she caught a glimpse of herself in the hallway mirror—her hair was a mess, bags under her eyes, and her face was ashen. She looked like a woman on the run. And she was.

Kyla shook her head, trying to clear her mind as she left the house. When she opened the door, someone stood on the porch outside—a figure. The sight made her gasp and drop the suitcase she was holding.

Part VI

Chapter 56

As I sat with Matt and the security guard in the dimly lit room, the only sound was the soft hum of the hospital machinery. The guard clumsily fiddled with the controls as he pulled up the surveillance footage on the screen. He was a scruffy-looking man in his forties who was in charge of hospital security. The three of us were huddled around a small monitor, trying to make sense of the surveillance footage that played before us.

It wasn't easy.

I leaned forward, peering intently at the monitor, searching for any clue that could help us solve the mystery of who had attacked John in his hospital bed. My heart raced with anticipation, and a knot formed in my stomach as I watched the footage. How was this even possible? How could this person get away with it so easily?

"I don't see anyone," the security guard said while going through the camera from the entrance and the front desk. "I mean, I see people coming and going, but it's late at night, not many visitors at this hour."

I still wondered how the heck this person made it through the front desk. Emily hadn't been able to. I asked the lady sitting there, and she said she hadn't seen anyone or let anyone go up to his room.

"Could it have been Parker? Rachel's dad?" Matt asked. He was sitting next to me, helping me look for the possible killer.

"It could," I said. "It's actually not a bad theory. We know he escaped from prison recently and, in a spectacular way, climbed up between two walls. Do you think he killed him? As revenge for his daughter? Maybe he found a way to get in where cameras didn't see him, or he didn't have to face the front desk. Maybe a back way?"

"Or maybe he climbed the freaking wall," Matt said and laughed. "You know... like Spiderman."

I nodded. It was possible; it could have been him. It had been all over the news that John Baker was the main suspect in Rachel's murder. Maybe he decided to take matters into his own hands.

It made sense.

I kept watching the monitor. Still, there was nothing but the usual comings and goings of hospital staff. But then, a slim figure appeared in the corner of the screen. It was hard to tell who it was, but the person seemed to be wearing a hooded sweatshirt with the hood pulled tightly over their head. They moved with a strange, almost mechanical precision as if they had rehearsed their movements beforehand. This person walked through the sliding doors, then walked to the chairs and sat down. A few seconds later, the person got up and walked past the cameras, then disappeared from view. A few seconds later, the same person stormed past the cameras and out into the night, running faster than their legs seemed to be able to keep up.

"What on earth?" I said. "Please go back and let me see that person again."

The security guard scrolled back, and we watched it again. Then, one more time, just to be certain.

"I know who that is," I said and rose to my feet. "That hooded sweater looks awfully familiar."

Chapter 57

I stood in the parking lot, the shadows of flat-roofed buildings looming over me. It was midnight, and the air felt thick with tension. I shivered as a gust of wind blew past me, not because it was cold but because it startled me. I was glad to have Matt with me, and feeling his presence right behind me made me calm. My footsteps echoed in the silence of the night as I approached a dilapidated old minivan, its paint peeling off in chunks. I hesitated before knocking on the door. It was dark and humid outside, and the rusted minivan looked like it was about to fall apart. I could hear my heart pounding as I knocked on the door.

"Janet? Janet, are you in there?" I called out, my voice shaking slightly. I waited for a few moments, but there was no answer. I knocked again, harder this time. "Janet, please. I need to talk to you."

A low moaning sound broke the silence. I couldn't tell if it was coming from the minivan or somewhere else in the lot. It could have been one of the stray cats or maybe a raccoon. I felt a shiver run down my spine, but I tried to keep my composure.

"Janet, I know you're in there," I said, louder this time. "It's

Agent Eva Rae Thomas and Matt Miller from Cocoa Beach Police. We need to talk to you. Please."

The door creaked open, and Janet peered out, her face twisted in anger. "I told you to go away!" she spat, her eyes flashing in the dim light.

I could see that she was agitated and frightened. Her hair was unkempt, and she had huge dark circles under her eyes. She was wearing a dirty old hoodie that was two sizes too big for her, and her hands were shaking.

"Janet, we just want to ask you a few questions," I said, trying to keep my voice calm and steady.

"I don't know anything! I swear!" Janet shrieked, her voice rising in hysteria. "Leave me alone!"

"Janet, please, we're not here to hurt you. We just want to help you," I said, taking a step closer to her.

"Go away! I don't want to talk to anybody," Janet yelled from inside the camper.

I could hear the fear and anxiety in her voice, and it worried me. I knew something was wrong, but I couldn't put my finger on what it was. I exchanged a nervous look with Matt and then spoke again.

"We just have...."

Janet suddenly slammed the door shut with a loud bang.

"Janet, I know you were at the hospital tonight. I saw you on the cameras," I yelled. "You went there to use the bathroom, didn't you? You go there from time to time to get washed up and use the restroom. You go when it's quiet there, and no one will notice. It's okay; there's nothing wrong with that. I just... well, I think you saw someone there tonight—someone who scared you because you've seen the person before. When they brought the body here and placed it in unit 203, am I right?"

There was no response from inside the minivan, but I could

hear the sound of footsteps shuffling around. Then, the door creaked open slowly, revealing Janet's disheveled appearance.

I smiled, relieved. "Janet, I need your help. Who was it you saw today? The one that scared you so much you had to run out of the hospital? Can you describe this person to me?"

Janet stared at me, her eyes growing wide and crazy. Then she lifted her hand and started hitting herself. "Stupid, stupid...."

"No, no, no," I said and grabbed her wrists to stop her. "Please, Janet. This is very important."

Janet looked at me with a wild-eyed expression. "I... I don't know. I don't remember," she stammered, her voice trembling with fear.

I could see the terror in her eyes, and my heart went out to her. I knew she was scared, but I also knew that she had valuable information that could help solve this case.

"Janet, I need you to focus. You saw something today, didn't you? Something that scared you. Please try to remember. It's important," I urged her gently.

Janet closed her eyes, and I could see her struggling to recall what had happened. After a few moments, she opened her eyes, and her face contorted with fear once again.

"It's that damn song again," she said, tilting her head. "It won't leave my head."

And then she started humming. I let go of her wrists, disappointed. I had really thought I had a lead this time, but Janet wasn't a reliable witness. There was nothing more I could do.

"Let's go home," Matt said and put a hand on my shoulder. "It's getting late."

Chapter 58

As we entered the house, I dropped my purse on the floor, went upstairs, and slumped down on the bed. The day had been so exhausting and stressful that I couldn't wait to just crawl under the covers and sleep. I got ready for bed, then heard Matt's footsteps approaching, and soon, he appeared in front of me, a mischievous look in his eyes.

"Hey, babe," he said, leaning down and planting a soft kiss on my lips. He crawled into bed with me, naked.

I smiled weakly and leaned into his embrace. His scent was comforting, but I was too tired to reciprocate his affection.

Matt sensed my lack of enthusiasm and pulled away. "What's wrong?" he asked, concern etched on his face.

"I don't know," I sighed, "I'm just so tired and depressed. I can't deal with anything right now."

Matt nodded understandingly and kissed me again. "I get it, babe. You don't have to explain. Just rest, and I'll take care of you."

He started massaging my shoulders, working out the knots that had accumulated throughout the day while I pondered about the case and tried to lift the guilt I was feeling for having failed to protect John Baker. I couldn't stop thinking about what this meant. He wasn't our suspect, after all? Or had someone killed him because he killed Rachel? Seeing how scared Janet was, I was so sure she had seen the killer there at the hospital. But it was hard to get anything out of her, anything useful, that was.

Matt's touch was gentle but firm, and I felt myself relaxing under his ministrations. I closed my eyes and let out a contented sigh.

As he worked his way down my back, his hands drifted lower, tracing delicate patterns along my skin. I shivered as he reached my lower back, his fingers brushing against my curves. I had lost a lot of weight this past year and was pretty content with my body as it was right now, even though I was still bigger than I used to be.

"Matt," I murmured, turning over to face him.

He grinned down at me, his eyes glinting with mischief. "What's wrong, baby?"

"Nothing's wrong," I said, my voice low and sultry. "I just want you to make me forget about everything else."

He leaned down to kiss me again, his lips soft and warm against mine. Then he began to trail kisses down my neck, his hands roaming over my body. He moaned in my ear, and it almost sounded like a song.

As Matt's hands started to trail down my body, I suddenly sat up, gasping for air. The song that Janet had been humming earlier suddenly came back to me, and I knew what it meant. How had I missed it?

"Matt, stop," I said, pushing him away. "I have to go. I have to solve this case."

"What? What's going on?" Matt asked, confused and concerned.

"I know what the song means, and I know who our killer is," I said, grabbing my clothes and rushing out of the room.

I quickly got dressed and headed out to my car, my heart racing with excitement and fear. I knew I was close to solving the case, but I also knew that the killer was dangerous, and I had to act fast. Matt complained but came running out behind me, still putting his shirt back on.

"Where are we going?" he panted as we got into the police cruiser.

"Kyla Johnson's house.

"Kyla? Rachel's sister? Why?" he asked as I accelerated out of our neighborhood and into the night.

"Because she's done it before. I read it in her file; she was accused of murdering before, but then someone else was convicted for it."

Chapter 59

Kyla stood on the porch of her house, her suitcase lying beside her. The darkness of the night enveloped her like a shroud, and a chill crept up her spine. The night air was still and heavy; the darkness seemed to be alive with a strange energy that made her shiver as it brushed against her skin. She could feel the weight of the world pressing down on her shoulders, and she couldn't shake the feeling that everything was about to fall apart.

"M-mom?" she called out, her voice trembling. "What are you doing here?"

Her mother emerged from the darkness, her brow creased with worry. Her shoulders were tight with tension, and her mouth was set in a thin line as she spoke. "You were about to make a mistake," she said, her words heavy with apprehension. "I couldn't let you do it."

Kyla's eyes filled with tears, and she could feel her heart rate go up rapidly. "B-but...."

Her mom stepped closer to her, her voice brittle and shaking. Kyla's face reddened, and her eyes focused on the floor. She couldn't force herself to make eye contact with her mom. A lump formed in her throat, and she felt like the room was spinning.

Her mother advanced slowly toward her, disappointment written all over her features. "No buts. You were going to leave, weren't you? Just take off like I meant nothing to you and leave your life behind—leave me behind even though you knew what that would do to me—how it would make me feel. Like I hadn't even been enough for you."

Kyla hung her head, feeling the weight of her mother's words crawl through her body. She couldn't deny it—she had been about to leave—leave everything behind and start anew. It seemed like the only option, the only path she could take to escape the pain.

But now, with her mother standing before her, Kyla felt a different kind of pain—the pain of guilt and shame. She had never meant to hurt her mother. She had never meant to make it seem like she didn't matter.

"I'm sorry," Kyla whispered, the words barely audible.

"You don't have to apologize," her mother said, reaching out to take Kyla's hand. "I understand the pain you're going through. But running away isn't the answer. You have to face your problems head-on, no matter how difficult it may be."

Kyla nodded, tears streaming down her face. She knew her mother was right. She shouldn't run away.

Her mother wrapped her arms around her, holding her close. "I'm here for you, always," she whispered in her ear. "We'll get through this together."

Kyla felt a sense of relief wash over her. She wasn't alone. She had her mother by her side, and she knew that with her support, she could face anything.

Taking a deep breath, Kyla wiped away her tears and picked up her suitcase. "Thank you, Mom," she said, looking up at her with a smile.

Her mother smiled back at her, her eyes brimming with pride. "That's my girl," she said, giving Kyla's hand a gentle squeeze. "Let's go inside and talk. Now remember, Rachel was going to leave too, and I told her, whatever you do, you can never ever leave. We are a family. Only death can part us."

Then, she closed the door behind them and locked it with a loud click. The sound was sharp and final.

Chapter 60

As I turned the car onto the street, I could feel my heart beating rapidly. Matt was sitting beside me, his hands tightly gripping his gun as we approached the house.

I shook my head, my eyes fixed on the house in front of us. My grip on the steering wheel tightened as I leaned forward, the adrenaline already pumping through my veins.

"Please, just tell me what's going on," Matt asked, his hand hovering over the gun on his lap.

"I can't," I said, my voice low and urgent. "We don't have time. Just trust me on this."

I stepped out of the car, my eyes scanning the quiet suburban street. It was dark, but the streetlights cast an eerie glow on the houses lining the road.

Matt followed me, his footsteps echoing against the pavement. I could hear the distant sound of police sirens and knew our backup was on their way.

I raised my gun, my hand steady as I approached the front door of the house. Matt did the same, his eyes darting around nervously.

"Ready?" I asked, keeping my voice low.

Matt nodded, his jaw set in determination. Together, we kicked open the door and rushed in.

The inside of the house was just as dark as the street outside, but I could hear the sound of footsteps coming from upstairs. I motioned for Matt to follow me as we cautiously made our way up the stairs, our guns at the ready.

As we reached the top of the stairs, we saw the door to the master bedroom was slightly ajar. I nodded at Matt, and we approached the door slowly.

As we pushed it open, I could see the mother, Madeline Johnson, kneeling on the bed. In her hand was a bloody knife, and she was repeatedly stabbing her daughter, Kyla, who was lying on the bed, whimpering for help.

Matt's eyes widened in horror as he rushed toward Madeline. "Stop!" he yelled, tackling her to the ground. The knife clattered across the room, and I rushed over to Kyla's side.

"Are you okay?" I asked, my voice gentle as I tried to assess her injuries.

Kyla was gasping for air, her eyes wide in terror. "Please, help me," she whispered, her voice barely audible over the sound of Madeline's thrashing.

I could feel my heart pounding as I tried to calm Kyla down. "It's okay," I said softly. "We're here to help you."

Meanwhile, Matt was struggling to subdue Madeline. She was fighting fiercely, but Matt was able to keep her pinned down for a few seconds. Suddenly, she broke free and grabbed the bloody knife from the floor. With one swift motion, she plunged it into Matt's side, causing him to scream in pain.

I could feel my heart racing as adrenaline surged through my body. With a trembling hand, I raised my gun and fired a shot at Madeline, but it only grazed her shoulder. She got up and ran toward me, grabbing the gun from my hand and pointing it at me.

"Get away from my daughter," she hissed, her eyes wild with rage. "She's mine. She always has been."

I backed away, my hands raised in surrender. "Please, Madeline," I said, my voice shaking. "We can help you. Just put down the gun."

But Madeline was beyond reason. She was panting heavily, her eyes fixed on me with a crazed intensity. I could feel my breath getting caught in my throat. I tried to back away, but she came closer. I could see the madness in her eyes as she pointed my gun at my head.

"Please, Madeline," I gasped, trying to reason with her. "We can talk about this. Just put down the gun."

But Madeline wasn't listening. She was panting heavily, her finger on the trigger.

I froze as Madeline's eyes locked onto mine, her grip on the gun tightening. I could hear Matt groaning in pain behind me, and I knew I needed to act fast.

"Madeline," I said, my voice calm and steady despite the fear pulsing through my veins. I could hear the sirens as backup came closer. "Put the gun down. It's over."

Madeline's eyes narrowed, and I could see the madness in them. "It's not over until I say it's over," she snarled, her finger tightening on the trigger.

I took a step forward, my hands raised in surrender. "Okay, okay. Just put the gun down. Let's talk about this."

Madeline hesitated for a moment, and at that moment, I saw my chance. I lunged forward, trying to wrestle the gun from her grip, but she was strong, and she fought back with fury.

We tumbled to the ground, Madeline's weight pressing down on me. I felt the cold barrel of the gun against my temple, and I knew that this was it—the end.

I closed my eyes and prepared myself when the door suddenly sprang open, and a figure emerged from the darkness.

Chapter 61

Parker burst into the bedroom with his heart pounding in his ears. He took in the scene before him: Madeleine standing by the window, her face illuminated by moonlight streaming through the glass, her hand tightly gripping a gun. His eyes darted to the finger curled around the trigger.

The scene before him was horrific. On the floor in front of Madeleine sat a woman on her knees, arms over her head to form a protective shield as if she could keep the bullet from hitting her that way. She was shivering as if she were trying to make herself invisible. The man on the floor nearby was on his back, clutching his bloody midsection and groaning in agony. And on the bed, blood pooled around her still body and eyes staring lifelessly into an unseen world, was a young woman with a face twisted in pain.

Kyla!

Parker's feet hit the ground with a thud, and he lunged toward Madeleine, arms outstretched. Before she had time to react, his hands were on her waist—twisting her body around as they tumbled back. The gun slipped from her grasp, and all the breath was knocked out of her lungs. They fought hard for control as Parker tried to pry the weapon away from Madeleine forcefully.

Parker felt Madeleine's weight against him as they spun and rolled across the floor. He could feel her muscles straining against his as they fought for possession of the gun. His heart thundered in his ears as he strained to keep her hands away from it. Every breath she exhaled was hot against his skin.

Parker grasped the gun with both hands, his knuckles turning white as he pulled against her grip. His face was scrunched in determination, and sweat was trickling down the side of his face. With a final effort, he yanked it free and immediately rolled away from her. He spun around, jumping to his feet, raised the gun, and aimed it directly at her.

"P-Parker?" she said. "What the heck are you doing?"

"Stopping you. Ending what I should have years ago."

"You don't know what you're talking about," Madeleine said. "You can't just come in here... all...."

"Oh, yes, I can," he said, moving closer with the gun. Madeleine stopped talking as she stared down the barrel of the gun.

The woman on the floor looked up at him, and he realized she was police when he saw her badge on her belt. That made him nervous. Cops always made him anxious.

"Stay down," he said to her as she tried to get up. He didn't trust her or the guy in the pool of blood.

She obeyed.

"Now, what the heck is going on here?" he asked. He glared at the lifeless body on the bed. He gasped when he saw how deep her stab wounds were. He grabbed her hand.

"Kyla, sweetie. Kyla, it's your daddy. I'm here."

Kyla answered with a deep moan. It barely sounded human. Anger rose in him when he saw this, and he walked to Madeleine and pressed the gun hard against her head.

"I ought to kill you right here and now."

"Please, don't," she pleaded, "please, don't."

"Give me one good reason not to," he said. "Just one!"

"Because of the grandchildren," she said. "Our grandchildren. Who is going to take care of them?"

"Oh, because their mothers are gone because you murdered them, you sick woman! What kind of mother kills all her own daughters? The first one when she was only nine years old, remember her?"

Chapter 62

THEN:

The day they were brought home was like a dream come true. Emma and Lily clung to their mother's hand, their hearts overflowing with joy and relief. It had been a difficult few weeks with their mother hospitalized and the girls placed in temporary foster care.

As they walked through the front door of their small house, Emma and Lily breathed in the familiar scent of home. The living room was filled with balloons, flowers, and cards from well-wishers, their mother's smile beaming with gratitude.

"Welcome home, my girls," their mother said, tears of joy streaming down her cheeks. "I missed you so much."

Emma and Lily hugged their mother tightly, feeling the warmth of her embrace and the reassurance that she was okay. They had been so worried about her, and it had been hard being apart from each other in different foster homes.

Their mother led them to the kitchen, where a feast of their favorite foods awaited them. Emma and Lily's eyes widened in delight as they saw the spread of chicken nuggets, mac and cheese, and chocolate cake.

"Mom, this is amazing!" Lily exclaimed, her mouth already watering.

"I wanted to make sure my girls had a proper homecoming feast," their mother said with a smile.

As they sat down to eat, Emma and Lily couldn't help but feel a sense of relief wash over them. They were finally back together with their mother, safe and sound. It was a feeling they had missed dearly.

"Mom, when are Elyse and Rachel coming?" Emma asked, eager to see her younger sisters.

"They'll be here soon; don't worry," their mother reassured her. She touched her big belly gently, then said, "And then Kyla will be here in about a month or so."

As they finished their meal, Emma and Lily could feel the exhaustion from the day's events starting to set in. They were grateful for their warm beds and the safety of their home.

"Good night, my loves," their mother said, tucking them in. "I'm so happy to have my girls back home with me."

"Goodnight, Mom," Emma and Lily replied in unison, their eyes already heavy with sleep.

As they began to drift off, their mother walked over and grabbed Emma's pillow. She gently fluffed it, then looked at both girls lovingly.

"My loves," she said softly, tilting her head, "there is one thing I want you both to take away from what we've been through. I want you always to remember that we are a family, and no one gets to leave us. Only death can part us."

Lily could barely comprehend the words her mother had uttered, and she watched with terror as their mother leaned over Emma in bed and slowly began to press the pillow down over her head. Emma thrashed beneath her, desperate for air as their mother began to press down forcefully with both hands. Every second felt like a lifetime until, finally, Emma lay still. The room seemed to spin around Lily as she looked at her sister's lifeless body in shock. Lily screamed, her voice reverberating through the room as she realized what had happened. Tears streamed down her face as she looked up at her mother, horror coursing through her veins.

"Now, do you understand?" their mother said coldly.

Lily merely nodded, too stunned to do anything else.

Their mother then wiped away a tear and quietly left the room, leaving Lily alone with Emma's corpse.

Chapter 63

"Lily never spoke about that day until she became a teenager," Parker said, his eyes glaring down at Madeleine. I was staring at him, shocked at the story unfolding. Who in their right mind would murder a child? Their own child?

"Lily was the one who called the cops, but when they got there, she didn't tell them the whole truth—only that Emma had died in her bed. She didn't dare say anything else; she was so scared of you. She told me this many years later, along with all the terrors you put them through, and that's when I came to you and told you I wanted the girls. I was going to sue for custody of all four of them. But you managed to stop me, didn't you?"

She snorted angrily. "You were going to take my girls away. No one leaves me—no one."

"You murdered Lily when she was just fourteen years old, stabbed her for wanting to live with me, and then you put the bloody knife in my apartment and told the cops to come for me, that I had murdered my own daughter in cold blood. You played the victim and led them in my direction. No one believed me because I had a prior from the time I tried to talk sense into you and tell you that you were being too harsh on the girls. You called the cops on me, and they took me away, and then you took out a restraining order on me, claiming I was a danger to my own children. After that, I couldn't see them or even come near them anymore. But you wanted it that way. You wanted them to yourself, and then when they grew older, you manipulated and threatened them to stay close to you. Kyla, Elyse, and Rachel all did. But Rachel wanted to leave, and you found out. She called me and said she wanted to move far away, and I sent her the money for the tickets. I prayed she would be able to get away before you could get your claws into her. But she didn't. You killed her, didn't you? So she wouldn't leave you. And then you made it look like it was her husband because he had cheated on her, and somehow, you were able to put the blame on him."

"The clothes," I said. They both looked at me. "That's why they didn't have his DNA on them. You put a bag of Rachel's bloody clothes in John's house with the pizza crust taken from his trash. You put it in the pocket of the pants, thinking it would somehow make his DNA present enough to incriminate him. And you made sure to put the body in his storage unit so he would automatically become a suspect. But there was a song that you hummed, both while dragging Rachel's body to the storage unit and after murdering John in the hospital, and a homeless woman recognized it. I immediately knew it was you by then, as soon as I understood what song it was. It was *Billie Jean* by Michael Jackson, your favorite singer. It's quite the earworm, isn't it? Once it gets stuck in your head, it just won't leave. But the homeless woman in the parking lot heard you. She couldn't see who you were, but she could hear that song, and it scared her. I guess you buried Elyse's body as well? The grave in the backyard was fresh. Why did Elyse have to die? Was she about to leave as well?"

"Yes," Madeleine hissed. "She had found some guy online in Spain who she desperately wanted to visit. I couldn't let her go. I knew she might stay there if she did, and then she would be gone. I would never see her again."

"So, you murdered her instead?" I asked, shaking my head in disbelief.

"No one leaves me—no one!" she spat at me.

"So, how did you do it? How did you kill Rachel?"

She stared at us. Parker moved closer with the gun, then yelled, "Tell her how you did it!!!"

"All right, geez, get that thing out of my face first," she said, and Parker took one step back.

'Then start talking."

Madeleine continued: "I waved her down. Knowing Rachel would go that way to the airport and knowing she was about to leave because I had seen the tickets on her computer, I placed myself on the side of the road, parked my car, and pretended to be in distress. Once she stopped, I told her my car had broken down and my phone was dead. She got into my car, then I slammed my fist into her temple, and she passed out."

"So that's what our witness saw," I said. "The two of you in your car, not Rachel's. I guess she failed to tell us there were two cars on the side of the road at the time. Please continue. What happened next?"

"I took off, leaving her car there to be found. I drove to work and parked behind the building, where I knew no one would see me. I put plastic covers on the seats so they wouldn't get blood on them. Then, I stabbed her inside my car—just one quick stab. Later, once it was dark, I took her to the storage unit and put her inside the barrel of formaldehyde I had bought. I once dated a mortician and knew it took only two liters of that stuff to embalm a body. You weren't supposed to find her until later when I had gotten rid of Elyse and saved my grandson from her, so I had to hurry. I wanted John to take the fall for both. I made sure to steal his necklace and put it on the ground outside. You must understand that I did it for the children's sake. Elyse had already had one divorce, and she was about to start all over with a new man, and I couldn't let her. I couldn't let her take Charlie away to some foreign country, and I couldn't lose her. Rachel was about to leave hers in the hands of John. I thought the children deserved more stability. They needed me."

"So, you were about to murder both of them in cold blood," I said. "That was probably why Elyse was calling Rachel at night. Maybe she knew something was up and wanted to warn her. But then she chickened out? Because she was scared? Had you threatened her?"

"No, I just told her she couldn't leave. She knew that. They both did. There is no leaving me. The girls know. I have said it their entire lives."

Parker sniffled and wiped his nose. He shook his head. "And what about poor Kyla? Look at her. Look at her, woman, and what you've done to her."

He grabbed her chin and forced her to look at her daughter in the pool of blood on the bed. I could hear more sirens, and they were getting close now. The sound of them made Parker look up for one unforgivable second, and that's when Madeleine grabbed her chance. With a sudden burst of strength, Madeleine pushed herself up from the floor and lunged for the gun. Her fingers grasped the metal, and for a moment, it looked like she might succeed, so I yelled to alert Parker. I jumped to my feet to help him, but as she pulled the gun toward her, there was a deafening bang.

Madeleine's body jolted back, and her grip on the gun slackened. Parker's eyes widened in horror as he saw the bullet wound in her chest. Madeleine's body crumpled to the floor, and Parker sank to his knees next to her.

Parker stared at her lifeless body, a mixture of shock and regret washing over his face. He slowly put the gun down and sat on the edge of the bed, his head in his hands. "I can't believe I just did that."

"It's okay," I said. "Just hand me the gun, please."

He let it drop to the floor, and I picked it up.

Just then, the sound of the door being smashed down echoed through the house, immediately followed by the pounding of heavy boots on the wooden steps leading to the upper floor. My heart raced as I hurried to Matt, who lay motionless on the floor, blood seeping from a wound in his side. I put pressure on the wound to stop the bleeding. He had already lost a lot of blood and was barely conscious.

The SWAT team from the sheriff's office burst into the room, their guns drawn and pointed at us. I held up my badge, trying to steady my voice, and shouted, "FBI! Don't shoot! That man on the floor is my partner; he's with CBPD, and he's been stabbed! I'm the one who called for backup."

The officers hesitated for a moment, their eyes flicking back and forth between us before lowering their weapons. One of them stepped forward, his gun still at the ready, and demanded, "What's going on here?"

I struggled to keep my voice calm as I explained the situation briefly, then added: "I need two ambulances ASAP. Someone should tend to the woman on the bed, please. And please, save my partner. Please."

Chapter 64

Matt's hand was slipping away from mine as the ambulance rushed us to the hospital. His face was pale, his eyes closed, and his breathing was shallow. I couldn't help but feel dizzy and nauseous as I watched the paramedics frantically try to stabilize him.

"We're losing him!" one of them shouted, his voice echoing in my head. "We need to get him to the hospital now!"

I clutched Matt's hand, pleading with him to stay with me. "Please, don't leave me," I whispered, tears streaming down my face. "You can't leave me like this."

The ambulance screeched to a stop at the hospital's emergency entrance. I stumbled out of the back of the ambulance, my mind racing with a million different thoughts. What if he doesn't make it? How will I live without him? I couldn't bear the thought of losing him.

The hospital staff rushed over to us, pushing the gurney with Matt's motionless body into the emergency room. I followed closely behind them, a desperate look on my face.

"Please, save him," I begged, my voice hoarse with emotion. "He's lost so much blood. Please, do something."

The doctors and nurses rushed around Matt, hooking him up to various machines and IVs. I stood there, feeling helpless and lost. It was all happening so fast, and I couldn't keep up with the chaos around me.

Suddenly, Matt's heart monitor started beeping rapidly, the sound filling the room with a sense of urgency. The doctors and nurses started to work even faster, their movements more frantic than before.

"He's going into cardiac arrest," one of them yelled. "We need to shock him!"

I could feel my heart racing as they shocked Matt's body multiple times, trying to bring him back to life. It was a scene straight out of a nightmare, and I couldn't believe it was happening to us.

After what felt like an eternity, Matt's heart monitor started beeping steadily, and the doctors and nurses let out a collective sigh of relief. They continued to work on him, their focus unwavering as they fought to save his life.

I collapsed into a chair, my head in my hands, my body shaking. Everything around me felt surreal—like I was watching a movie. But as I looked up at Matt's motionless body, I knew that this was all too real.

Hours passed, and the doctors and nurses continued to work tirelessly to keep Matt alive. Every beep of the machines, every frantic movement, sent me into a panic. But despite my fear and desperation, I refused to leave his side.

Finally, after what felt like an eternity, the doctors emerged from the emergency room, their faces grim but relieved.

"He's stable," one of them said, putting a hand on my shoulder. "We managed to stop the bleeding and stabilize him. But the nerves of his leg were damaged, and there's a blockage of the arteries supplying the leg, meaning that the blood circulation has been severely reduced. There's no longer enough blood to keep the leg alive. We will need to amputate."

The doctor's words hit me like a ton of bricks. Amputate? Was he really suggesting that they cut off Matt's leg? Wasn't there another way?

I stared at the doctor, my mind racing with a million different thoughts. How would Matt cope with losing a limb? Would he ever be able to walk again? Would his life ever be the same?

The doctor must have seen the fear in my eyes because he put a hand on my shoulder and said, "It's going to be okay. We can fit him with a prosthetic leg, and he'll learn how to use it."

I nodded, trying my best to stay calm. He was right. This was by far the best option for Matt, and if it meant saving his life, then I had no choice but to accept it.

"Okay, then, as long as he will come home with me, and we can be a family again."

The doctor nodded and placed a hand on my shoulder. "Of course."

Then he left, and I stood there in the cold waiting room, my heart heavy with worry and fear for the future. But despite it all, I knew I would never give up on Matt. I would do anything to ensure his recovery and bring him back home to me and our family. Nothing was more important right now.

Chapter 65

Finally, after many long hours, a nurse approached me with a slight smile on her face. "You can see him now," she said, motioning for me to follow her.

I took a deep breath and followed her down the hallway to Matt's room. He was lying in the hospital bed, his eyes closed, but I could see his chest rising and falling slowly. I approached him, taking his hand in mine.

"Hey," I whispered, my voice cracking with emotion. "You scared me, you know that?"

Matt's eyes fluttered open, and he looked up at me with a weak smile. "Sorry," he said, his voice only a whisper.

I leaned down, pressing a kiss to his forehead. "Don't be sorry," I said. "Just promise me you'll never scare me like that again."

"I promise."

I smiled at him, tears in my eyes. "Kyla made it," I then said. "She was in critical condition for a long time, but they just told me she made it. So, we saved her from her mother's claws. That's something you can be proud of. And Parker went back to jail. He will try for a retrial, and I will testify that I heard the confession from Madeleine, and hopefully, he won't have to serve any more time in jail for what she did to her own daughter."

"And the children?" he said and winced in pain.

"I'm afraid they will probably all have to go into foster care. Unless Kyla will take them, but she will need months of recovery, and they need homes now. We'll have to see what happens there. Either way, they're safe."

As I held Matt's hand, I could sense the fear and sadness that was consuming him. I knew I had to be strong for him, but it was hard to see him in this state. His gaze shifted to his missing leg, and he turned back to me with a look of desperation.

"Did you know they took my leg?" he asked, his voice trembling.

I nodded, tears streaming down my face. "Yes, Matt. They had to. Your life was in danger, and they had to do what they could to save you."

He closed his eyes, tears rolling down his cheeks. "How will I be able to live my life now?" he whispered, his voice filled with despair. "How will I be a detective if I can't run or chase after suspects?"

I hugged him tightly, holding him close to me. "We'll figure it out, Matt," I said, my voice breaking. "We'll find a way to make it work. You're still the same smart and talented detective you've always been. We'll adapt and find other ways to catch the bad guys. And most importantly, you're alive. That's all that matters."

Matt sniffled, leaning his head on my shoulder. "I know you're right," he said, his voice muffled by my shirt. "But it's just hard to imagine my life without running and chasing. It was part of who I was."

"I know," I said, smoothing his hair back. "But you're so much more than that, Matt. You have so many other talents and skills that make you an amazing detective. We'll find a way to make it work. Together."

Matt looked up at me, his eyes red from crying. "Thank you," he said, his voice barely audible. "I don't know what I'd do without you."

I smiled, wiping away his tears. "You'll never have to find out," I said. "I finally have you, and there's no way I'm letting go of you again."

That made him laugh. It was a wonderful sound.

"You sound like Madeleine Johnson," he said.

I laughed, too, realizing he was right. "I guess that did sound kind of crazy, huh?"

"Sure did."

I kissed him and looked deeply into his eyes with a deep sigh. I guess the lesson we learned was that we never knew how long we would have the people we loved in our lives. It was all a matter of enjoying them while we still could.

THE END

The following pages will include an excerpt of the first book, **DON'T LET HER GO** in a new mystery series by Willow Rose featuring her new protagonist **detective Billie Ann Wilde.**

Afterword

Dear Reader,

Thank you for purchasing *Till Death Do Us Part (Eva Rae Thomas #14)*. The idea for this book came when a friend of mine had a cousin who disappeared after dropping the kids off at daycare. She wasn't found until two months later when she turned up dead. The story of Madeleine Kingsbury is strange and ugly, and you can read more here if you like:

https://www.foxnews.com/us/missing-minnesota-mom-madeline-kingsburys-family-feared-foul-play-disappeared-daycare-drop

https://www.dailymail.co.uk/news/article-12175121/Family-confirms-body-Madeline-Kingsbury-26-went-missing-two-months-ago.html

The story of the girls and their vicious mother is real, too. I found it in a Danish media outlet and read through it, then decided to write about something similar. No one was killed in their story; I just used it as an inspiration. It's in Danish, but if you want, you can try to look at it here:

https://fyens.dk/odense/naale-op-under-neglene-og-tvunget-til-at-slikke-toilet-og-gulv-soestre-staar-frem-og-fortaeller-om-uhyrlig-opvaekst-hos-deres-mor

Also, the escape from prison story was inspired by an actual event. Recently, a convicted murderer, Danelo Cavalcante, escaped from Chester County Prison in Pennsylvania by crabbing his way between two walls. He was on the run for two weeks before finally being brought back behind bars. You can read more about his escape here, which was also caught on video:

https://www.cnn.com/2023/09/12/us/danelo-cavalcante-escape-manhunt-timeline/index.html

As always, I want to thank you for all your support. Please leave a review if you can. Also, I have attached an excerpt from a new series I have been working on, which I am very excited to get out to you, my dear reader. This is the first sneak peek, so continue on if you want to read it.

Take care,

Willow

Join Willow Rose's VIP Newsletter to get exclusive updates about New Releases, Giveaways, and FREE ebooks.
Just scan this QR code with your phone and click on the link:

SCAN ME

Win a waterproof Kindle e-reader or a $125 Amazon giftcard!
Just become a member of my Facebook group **WILLOW ROSE -
MYSTERY SERIES.**
Every time we pass 1000 new members, we'll randomly select
a winner from all the entries.

To enter go here: https://www.facebook.com/groups/
1921072668197253

Tired of too many emails? Text the word: "willowrose" to 31996
to sign up to Willow's VIP text List to get a text alert with news
about New Releases, Giveaways, Bargains and Free books from
Willow.

Follow Willow Rose on BookBub here: https://www.bookbub.
com/authors/willow-rose

Follow Willow on BookBub

Connect with Willow online:
https://www.facebook.com/willowredrose
https://twitter.com/madamwillowrose
http://www.goodreads.com/author/show/4804769.Willow_Rose
https://www.willow-rose.net
Mail to: contact@willow-rose.net

Introduction

If you are desperate for more unputdownable thrillers from Willow Rose, get *Don't Let Her Go*, the first book in her brand new series featuring Detective Billie Ann Wilde. A missing five-year-old girl is the key to unlocking Billie's terrifying past in this heart-racing first installment in the series.

Get it here: https://geni.us/B0CNTVS39Wendmatter1
or read on for an exclusive extract...

Excerpt of DON'T LET HER GO
DETECTIVE BILLIE ANN WILDE 1

A missing five-year-old girl is the key to unlocking a detective's terrifying past...

Prologue

Cocoa Beach, Florida

Marissa Clemens smiled the way only a mother could when looking at her child. Her four-year-old daughter Emma was dancing in the backyard, while Marissa was cooking dinner inside the house, watching her through the kitchen window.

"Look at me, Mommy!"

Emma was wearing a tutu, and it spun in the air as she twirled. On her feet she was wearing pink Crocs, while her small legs were bare. On top she wore her favorite shirt, the one with glittery unicorns and rainbows on it. Marissa could tell that her daughter had worn it a lot, because most of the sparkles had fallen off. She wondered if she should get rid of it, but the girl loved it so much, she didn't dare to. Emma's strawberry blonde hair was tousled and curly and kept falling into her face. Her smile was the most beautiful on the planet and could melt any hardness in her mother.

"Look I'm dancing!"

The girl mimicked a video from YouTube that she had watched, featuring a group of young girls who were twerking, and it made her mother laugh, even if it was slightly inappropriate. Seeing a four-year-old do it was just too darn cute.

Marissa looked down at the potatoes she was peeling, allowing herself a brief moment of happiness. Could she finally relax? Were they safe?

What if things stayed good from now on?

She didn't dare believe it. Marissa shook her head. No, it was simply too dangerous to fill herself with that kind of hope.

"Mommy, Mommy, can I go down to the water?"

Marissa looked up with a drastic change in her expression. Her blissful smile became a frown, and she raised her finger and kept Emma's eye contact. She made sure her daughter looked at her and understood what she was saying.

"No. No going to the pond without Mommy."

"Please? I wanna see the fishies," Emma said, making those big begging eyes. It usually worked if Emma wanted snacks, but not when it came to this. The big pond behind their backyard was Marissa's nightmare. She had often dreamed of finding her floating in that water, and the very thought made her nauseated. She had sacrificed so much to get them to where they were. She wasn't taking any chances.

"No."

Emma made a sad face, but then spotted a squirrel as it darted across the lawn and decided to run after it, quickly forgetting everything about the pond. Marissa watched her as she talked to the small animal that had taken shelter on the top of the palm tree.

"Mommy, the squirrel is back," Emma yelled.

Marissa watched her for a few seconds, then finished peeling the potatoes. It was still scorching hot out even if it was October, and she had to make sure Emma drank enough water while playing outside. She put the potatoes in the buttered pan, then placed them in the oven after sprinkling cheese on top. She heard the washing machine play its annoying little song, letting her know it was done.

Marissa looked at her watch. She needed to put the clothes in the dryer, and, for that, she had to go to the garage. She hesitated. Should she ask Emma to come inside while she did it? No, that would be silly. She was having so much fun and getting fresh air.

Marissa walked to the garage and opened the lid of the washer. She started to pull out clothes and put them in the dryer. Emma would be fine. Besides, it would only take a few minutes to empty the washer and turn on the dryer. Five minutes at the most, she told herself. She emptied the washer and closed the dryer, while pushing back that intense nagging sense of urgency inside of her, telling her to go out and check on her daughter. She slammed the dryer shut and turned it on, then stared at the rest of the dirty laundry in the basket. She really needed to get another one going. There was time to put on another load, right? After all, it would only take another minute. Emma was fine. Of course, she was.

Marissa tossed the white wash into the washer, added detergent, and pushed the button to start. Happy that she was ahead of her own schedule for today, Marissa then rushed into the kitchen and peeked out the window.

But she couldn't see Emma.

There's no reason to panic. She's probably just playing somewhere I can't see. She's fine. Nothing can happen in a closed-in yard.

Heart throbbing in her throat, she grabbed a bottle of water from the fridge on the porch. She felt a humid blanket envelop her, as was usual in Florida when walking outside from the dry and cold air-conditioning inside. She took in a deep breath to calm herself down and felt sweat spring to her forehead immediately. That was Florida for you. You could get soaked in sweat from the brief minute it took to walk from your house to your car in the driveway.

"Emma?" she said. "I brought you some water, you need to remember to drink enough in order to stay..."

Marissa paused. She looked by the tree where she had last seen her daughter talk to the squirrel. But she wasn't there. She wasn't in the bushes behind it or on the porch. Then she turned to look toward the small grass area at the end of the yard, where Emma often liked to play, and where she had hosted a tea party earlier for her imaginary friends, but she wasn't there either.

"Emma?"

She could hear it in her own voice. The panic that was slowly spreading, eating her up from the inside, like a cancer.

"Emma?"

She rushed down the stairs, into the grass, and let her eyes frantically search for any sign of the little girl. Her voice was shrill as she yelled her name again and again, almost finding it hard to get the word across her lips because of the anxiety rushing through her slender body.

"Emma? Emma?"

Marissa ran to the end of the yard and stopped at the fence. She looked at the gate. It was still locked.

Marissa turned and looked at her small townhouse. Emma could perhaps be on the other side of the house. Marissa calmed down slightly. Of course, that's where she was.

Marissa ran up to the house, then went around it, and rushed into the front yard. She would have to get angry at Emma for doing this when she knew she wasn't allowed to. She might even have to put her in time-out. It wasn't that big a deal, but with the circumstances they lived under, Marissa couldn't be too careful. She couldn't risk a car driving by in the street and someone seeing the child.

Time-out it was. Just for ten minutes. Maybe she would serve ice cream for dessert after dinner, as compensation. To make her happy again. Yes, that would work. Marissa didn't like having to discipline her child.

"Emma? Emma, come here now. You know you're not allowed to..."

Marissa turned the corner of the house, then paused.

There was no sign of the girl in the front either.

Then where could she be?

Maybe she went back into the house? Maybe she ran inside just as you stormed outside?

It was getting harder for Marissa to calm herself down. She ran around the house and up the back patio, then hurried inside. Sweat was springing from her forehead and upper lip now, and not just because of the high humidity and heat. These were pearls of anxiety.

"Emma? Don't hide from me."

Her voice sounded angry, but it was hard to hide the fear.

"Please Emma? I don't have time for this, come here now."

She looked through the living room, then the kitchen and ran upstairs. She rushed into Emma's room, thinking she might be in there, playing, oblivious to her mother's panic attack. That she would be sitting on the floor and look up at her with those big, beautiful eyes, like she didn't understand what the urgency was about.

"Emma? Are you in here?"

She pushed the door open, but there were no eyes staring up at her. No cute smile or strawberry blonde hair falling into her daughter's eyes.

And there was no Emma.

"Emma?" she yelled. "EMMA?"

Could she have been...? Could it be...?

For a moment she dropped her face into her hands. *Don't think like that. I mustn't.*

She lifted her head, unable to stop her torso from shaking. She tried to calm her thoughts.

Think, Marissa. Think!

A small deep growl left her throat as she looked out the window and saw something in the grass. Something pink, left by the fence in the high grass that should have been mowed long ago. Marissa could barely breathe, and she held a hand to her mouth as the realization sank in of what it was she was looking at.

It was her shoes. Emma's pink shoes.

Chapter 3

BILLIE ANN

"You're an impostor. A liar."

I whispered the words to the woman staring at me from inside the mirror. To be honest, then I had no idea who she was anymore.

I was in my bathroom, naked after the shower, a towel still wrapped around my hair that had finally grown back to its old length. I stared at my chest and touched the scar where my left breast used to be. It felt strange. My right breast looked the same as it had always been, but I didn't trust it anymore. Anything could be growing in there. I had learned that the hard way.

It was three years ago today that I had been declared in remission. My latest checkup had shown the cancer hadn't come back. Still, the feeling never left the body. The first time they had told me it was cancer, it had come as such a big shock and had been so aggressive there was nowhere I really felt safe. No part of my body felt secure. It had deceived me. I had thought I was healthy, but my treacherous body had other plans.

It could come back. It could always come back. There would forever be that threat hanging over me. I was living with an expiration date. That's how it felt. And that had made me want to change things.

I needed to stop surviving and start living.

I reached into the drawer beneath the sink, then pulled out my husband's shaver. I took off the towel and threw it on the floor. Then I looked at the impostor with her long wet hair dangling from her head, sweeping across her shoulders.

It was time to get rid of her.

I turned on the shaver and placed it on the top of my head. I had done this once before, but for different reasons. Back then it had been because of the cancer, because I looked death in the eyes in the battlefield that was my body. Now it was because I had survived. I had won.

The shaver slid through the hairs like it was butter. It felt so satisfying, a smile grew on my face as I watched the big locks of curly blonde hair fall down into the sink. Last time I had seen that I had been so scared. Back then it had represented me losing control. Now I was taking it back.

And it felt great. No, it was more than that. It felt empowering.

I ran the shaver across my entire head, leaving just half an inch of hair all over. I wasn't going for bald, just a buzz cut.

When I was done, I stared at the woman in the mirror and smiled again. "There you are," I said to her, then cleaned the shaver and put it away. I studied my reflection once more and ran a hand across my head, feeling the short hair prickle the palm of it.

Then I got dressed. I found my black pants and button-down blue shirt, then put on my belt with my badge and my gun, that I retrieved from the safe. I looked at myself in the full body-sized mirror in my bedroom, and I felt good.

For once I looked like me.

I walked down the stairs, taking nervous but determined steps. I could hear my husband, Joe, and the kids in the kitchen.

My heart throbbed for a second as I walked in and all their chatter stopped.

"Whoa," my son, William, said. He had just taken a bite of his pancake and stared at me, mouth wide open. William was fourteen and as handsome as they get, but right then, he wasn't showing off his best side.

I smiled as casually as I could.

"What did you do?" he continued.

I touched my hair, or lack thereof. "This? You like it?"

"I think it looks badass," my sixteen-year-old daughter, Charlene, said, nodding her head acceptingly. "Buzz cuts are so in these days. You rock it, Mom. You look like Kristen Stewart in that movie we watched, where she's underwater."

"I think you look good too," my nine-year-old son, Zack, said without even looking up from his phone. He grabbed his cereal bowl and took it to the dishwasher. The two others stopped staring as well, as the news of my hair became uninteresting, and they left the kitchen to get ready for school. Now it was just me and Joe, and our golden retriever, Zelda, left in the kitchen. Joe stared at me, fighting his tears. His upper lip wobbled slightly.

I smiled compassionately at him.

He shook his head. "Why? Why would you do this?"

I shrugged. "I thought it was time for a change."

He nodded and looked down at the lunch boxes he was packing with peanut butter and jelly sandwiches. I bit my lip, feeling his sadness across the room. I approached him and touched his shoulder.

"It's gonna be okay."

He lifted his gaze, then touched my head gently, tears springing to his eyes. "You had just gotten all your hair back after..."

He paused.

"After the cancer. You can say it, you know?"

He nodded. "I know. But why would you cut it all off?"

"Listen, Joe. Change is going to come. For all of us."

He bit back his tears. My stomach began to hurt. I hated seeing him like this. I loathed myself for doing this to him.

"So... you're really going through with this?" he asked.

I exhaled. Tears were coming to my eyes too, but I fought them. "It's not gonna go away. These things don't go away."

He started to cry. It broke my heart, and I pulled him into a hug. He whispered between sobs.

"I don't want to lose you."

"Shh," I said, holding him. His six-feet-two and two hundred and twenty pounds were shaking in my arms. "You won't, sweetie. Things are going to change, yes, but I am still here. We have our kids together. We have been together for eighteen years. We'll figure things out, okay? It's a process. Both of us are in uncharted waters here. But there has to be a way."

He nodded and pulled away. "I'm sorry. This can't be easy for you either. I know it isn't. I'm just... I just don't understand. We've been married for this many years, we had a great life together, children, the works. I just keep thinking... how could you not have known that you were gay? Was everything we had just a lie?"

I sighed. This was all Joe had been able to focus on. "I guess I didn't want to know," I said, repeating the words he'd already heard me say. "Deep down I have always known. But I didn't want it to be true. It wasn't a lie, or maybe it was, sort of, but I was also lying to myself. That's why it is so hard. Because I can't ignore it anymore. I need to live out who I am. Be authentic. Life really is short. It's not just a cliché. We've learned this the hard way these past few years. I need this now."

He nodded again. I had told him all this the night before when I had sat him down over dinner for a talk. Just the two of us. It had taken me four years to get the courage to finally tell him this deep secret that I had kept from everyone my entire life. That I was gay.

I was attracted to women and always had been. But growing up the way I did with my religious parents, it simply wasn't an option. I had to marry a guy and have children. That was just the way it was. And so I did. I married a wonderful man who gave me three beautiful children. But I wasn't happy. I had this deep feeling inside that I was in the wrong place. Something was missing. I knew I was breaking his heart. We had promised each other we'd stay together forever. But now I just wasn't sure I had forever to give anymore. Time was running out, or so it felt at least. And I wanted to be me. Fully me. Even if it meant risking everything I had.

I needed this.

I'm gay. I'm a lesbian.

The words were still so hard for me to say, even to myself.

Once you let that toothpaste out of the tube, you can't get it back in again. It's as simple as that.

Even if it meant destroying everything I had built. My marriage, my family, maybe even my career. Would it be harder to climb the ranks? How were my colleagues going to react? Would they be disgusted by me and who I was? Cocoa Beach was a small beach town on a barrier island where everyone knew one another, and the locals were on a first name basis with many of the officers. Would I still gain the same respect among them? Among my coworkers? Or would coming out ruin all that?

My therapist had told me not to use words like *ruin* and *destroy*, because of their negative connotations. What I was doing was positive; I was finally becoming who I was meant to be. But it felt like I was ruining things. I had everything, and now I was throwing it all away.

There it was again, one of the words. *Throwing.* According to my therapist I was gaining a new life. That's what I needed to focus on. But that was so hard. I felt selfish. I felt like I was doing something wrong.

Yet now that I had told my husband, there was no way back.

Joe leaned forward and kissed my forehead. I could tell he was holding back tears.

"I love you so much, and I just want you to be happy. I'm just still a little... I'm finding it a little hard to grasp."

I swallowed, trying to get rid of the huge lump in my throat. I wanted to scream or run away or both at the same time. We barely slept all night. He was tossing and turning and getting up every half an hour, pacing back and forth. I knew it was a bomb I had thrown the night before. I knew he was still in shock and needed time to process it. Heck, so did I. Even if I had been dealing with it for years. It was still new territory for me, and I kept wondering if it was worth it.

"I know," I said. "It's gonna take some time for all of us to adjust."

"I just... I don't get it," he continued, sipping his coffee. His skin was gray from the lack of sleep. It was torture to watch him like this. He kept staring into blank air, repeating the same thing over and over again.

"I just don't get it..."

I couldn't blame him. While it had taken years for me to get to this point, his whole life had blown up in his face overnight.

So far, we had agreed to continue our normal lives and not talk to the children about it yet. Not till we knew how to deal with this situation. Not till we made any decisions that would affect their lives. I had told Joe about the numerous times I had ended up kissing girls when I was younger and had too much to drink. And that it had happened more recently...

Joe handed me a cup of coffee without looking at me. He had been my partner and best friend for eighteen years. Was that about to end? We hadn't been intimate for a long time, but we were a team. We were best friends. I would do anything not to lose him completely.

The kids came storming down the stairs, backpacks in hands, grabbed their lunches and took off while fighting over something ridiculous. I watched them from the window as they got into Charlene's Toyota pickup truck, which we got her for her sweet sixteen, and took off. I spotted our neighbors, Trevor and Marge, walking their goldendoodle on the sidewalk outside my window. Their dog, Sonny, stopped to pee by the tall palm tree in front of my house. I lived at the end of the cul-de-sac, which had been a very safe environment for my kids to grow up in. They would bike and skateboard around, and I never had to worry about them. Sonny did a little more than just pee, and Trevor bent down to pick it up. They were an elderly couple who had lived in Cocoa Beach their entire lives and never wanted to leave. "This is paradise but don't tell anyone because then they'll all want to come here too," they always said.

I waved at them. They waved back with big smiles in tanned faces. They were both very fit for their age. Marge did beach yoga every morning with her friends, and Trevor was an avid surfer. Our street was only two blocks from the beach, so he would get up at the crack of dawn and sometimes I would see him rushing down the street, barefoot, wearing nothing but boardshorts with his surfboard under his arm. That's when I knew the waves were good and most of the town would probably be out there in the lineup. Most of the neighbors on my street with only eight houses surfed or stand-up paddled on the river, some kayaked in the canals behind our houses. We all had boats by our docks in the backyards that we would occasionally go out on. It had been a while, though, since Joe and I had last been out on the water with the kids. They used to love it and would fight over whose turn it was to go in the tube, being pulled behind it. Or to go wakeboarding. That was fun. I chuckled at the memories we had created, then felt awful for my children. They had no idea what was about to happen to them, how their world was about to crumble, once their parents separated.

The very thought made me want to throw up.

"Can you take Zelda out?" I asked Joe, and he nodded quickly as I looked at my watch. "I'm running late for the morning meeting."

Chapter 4
OLIVIA

She was ahead of her target time. Olivia Thomson's Apple Watch told her so in her Air Pods. She had run the first kilometer in less than five minutes, and that was a good time for her. She was going for ten kilometers this morning, as she did three times a week, getting herself ready for the half-marathon she had signed up for in two months. Today she felt stronger than she had in a long time. She was almost flying as she ran through her neighborhood, her Salomon running shoes crunching on the pavement. In her ears she was listening to Pitbull, and the upbeat Latin rhythms made her go even faster. She wasn't usually a Pitbull fan, but she had found that when running, she was way faster while listening to his music.

When she reached two kilometers, her Apple Watch told her she had run the last kilometer at 04:45. It was a new record for her, and now she couldn't stop smiling.

Olivia had started running after her boyfriend of six years broke up with her. One day they had been on the couch, watching TV, when he paused the movie and simply told her he was leaving to be with her best friend of more than fifteen years.

She'd needed to get the anger out. It was piling up inside of her. Olivia wasn't good at showing emotions, especially not anger; instead, she would internalize it and that wasn't very healthy for her, her sister said.

"You need to yell at him. Get angry. Tell him how you really feel," she had told her over and over again.

But Olivia simply couldn't. She didn't feel like she was allowed to for some reason. She didn't like people seeing her being vulnerable. She needed people to think she was strong. After all she was an investment banker, one who had made it well for herself in a man's world. She couldn't lose her cool.

Besides, she wasn't going to give her ex the pleasure of seeing her angry or even sad. So instead, she had just watched him pack his stuff and leave, then decided never to talk to him or Katie again. It wasn't like she needed them or anything. She was very fine on her own.

Running had given her the outlet that she needed. When she pushed her body to its limits, that's when she was able to let it all out. The anger, the tears, the frustration. It would all come at once, and she could push through it, making her body ache so bad she was about to throw up.

Boy that made her feel good.

She ran the third kilometer in 04:35, her watch told her.

Olivia smiled widely. This was yet another record. She couldn't believe it. Usually, she would slow down on the third and fourth kilometer and struggle at the fifth, before picking up pace again on the sixth. But not today.

Today she was on fire.

Olivia turned a corner around the pink house, which she had always thought was so cute, then ran into another street and down toward the pond. There was such a nice little water fountain in the middle of it, making the entire neighborhood look expensive. It was beautiful. The houses with yards facing toward the pond were old and gorgeous. Olivia was always on the lookout for one of them coming up for sale, because she would love to buy one someday. Lord knows she had the money for it. But they rarely came up for sale.

"I'd really like that one," she mumbled to herself and pointed up at a small house with wraparound porches and the cutest little fenced-in yard. That one was her absolute favorite because it was so private. She had often tried to look into the yard when running past it on the trail surrounding the pond, but the tall bushes blocked her view. She liked that a lot.

"Privacy is king," she mumbled, then continued on her run. There was no slowing down now that she was doing so well. She would circle the pond, then go back. Once she made it halfway around it, she would hit five kilometers, and then she was halfway. Olivia took in a deep breath of fresh air. She could smell the ocean and the beach on the other side of A1A. She would occasionally run on the beach, but it was so darn hard on the knees when it wasn't low tide. She was scared of getting an injury and then where would that leave her? She needed to run. She was addicted to it, her sister had said. And maybe she was right.

It wasn't exactly the worst thing to be addicted to, was it?

Olivia shook her head with a scoff at the thought of her sister who couldn't get her own life together, and then she dared criticize Olivia's. Who did she think she was? Telling her she needed to grieve her loss and face her emotions.

It was all nonsense.

Olivia had her own way of dealing with things, and running was all she needed right now.

She ran the fifth kilometer in 04:40. Slower than the last one. She'd have to speed up, if she wanted to run her personal best, like she had been on track for. She wasn't going to slow down now.

Olivia accelerated, pushing her legs to the limit of what she was capable of, feeling her heart pound in her chest as she sprinted across the trail and around the pond. She turned for a second to look at the fountain in the middle, and how beautiful the rays of the sun hit it and created such a gorgeous light, when there was something else that caught her eye.

At first, she thought it was a gator. She had seen them occasionally in the pond, which wasn't a big deal, as they were in most ponds in Florida from time to time. But there was something about this floating mass that just struck her as odd.

It was sort of bobbing up and down below the surface.

Was it an animal?

Olivia stared at it as she came closer to where the lump was stuck in the mangrove bushes growing at the edge of the pond. She didn't even realize she had started to slow down till her watch suddenly said she was way behind her target pace.

But at this point, Olivia wasn't listening. She took out her Air Pods and stopped running. She stared at the small mass in the water, especially at the pink shirt bobbing on the surface.

Then she screamed.

Chapter 5

BILLIE ANN

"Billie Ann Wilde, as I live and breathe. What the heck did you do to your hair? You joining the Army or somethin'?"

Big Tom stopped himself, and his expression became serious. "Wait a second, you're not telling me that it's back, are you? Is the cancer back—?"

I raised a hand to prevent my colleague from saying something he would be embarrassed about later.

"I'm gonna stop you right there. It's not back," I said. "I'm still in remission."

He stared at me with his brown eyes. His handsome face smiled with relief. Tom was a big guy, hence the nickname, not as much in height as in volume—and character. He took up a lot of space in any room. He was very muscular and went to the gym several times a week, working out with the other guy in our division, Scott. I had recently been promoted to be the head of homicide, which basically meant the Chief left me in charge of these two goofballs. They were good people, and hard workers, and I loved them dearly, but they were also young and untrained, whereas I came with experience from another homicide division, not far from my hometown.

I grew up in Central Florida, out in the wetlands, fishing and hunting hogs and gators in the Green Swamp with the boys of my town. If I saw a snake, I knew not to tread on it, because it was my friend. If it snuck into my house, I knew how to grab it by the neck so it couldn't bite me and take it outside and let it go. My dad had taught me how to shoot a rifle from the moment I could hold one, and I was a better shot than both of my brothers. I knew how to deal with boys like Tom and Scott and had done so my entire life.

"Ha. You got me there. You got me good."

"I wasn't trying to but thanks," I said.

I sat down at my desk, across from Tom's, in the newly built police station in the center of downtown Cocoa Beach. It was a tall, ugly, square, gray building, and kind of an eyesore to this small quaint town with all the many beach houses and bungalows from the sixties and seventies. The space program had flourished then, and the town had grown to house the many workers at Kennedy Space Center.

The old building before this one had a leak in the roof after a hurricane, and mold was growing on the walls and floors. If a big rainstorm came by, and they did for most of the rainy season in summer, at least once a day, it would literally rain inside too. The AC was old and barely working, and on hot summer days we would be sweating like pigs inside of it. It was really no wonder we enjoyed this new modern building, even if it was very ugly.

"So, what's with the hair then?" Tom asked, sipping his big YETI cup that I knew contained a protein shake, his first of at least four that he would devour in a workday.

"I mean not that you don't look dashing," he added with a wink. "You always do."

I shrugged and touched my hair. "I don't know. I kind of liked it short and missed it, I guess. Besides it's too hot to have long hair in Florida."

I smiled awkwardly while secretly scolding myself. This was an opportunity for me to tell him the truth. I mean I had to do it at some point, right? I had to tell them all. But I feared so badly I would lose their respect for me. It just didn't feel like the right time.

Was there ever going to be a right time to say something like that?

Just get it over with. Say it!

I took in a deep breath and looked at my two colleagues. Tom was staring at his computer screen, probably flipping through emails, before this morning's meeting. Scott was on the phone, his soft black curls bouncing on his forehead as he spoke.

"Tom?"

"Mm-hm?" he said without looking away from his screen.

"There's... there's kind of something I need to tell you."

He sipped his big protein drink, then looked at me. "What's up? You look so serious?"

"I'm... I wanted to tell you that Joe and I... I mean I am..."

I couldn't even look at him as I babbled on. I was making no sense, I knew that, but I couldn't figure out how to say it right.

"What's going on with you and Joe?" he asked with a frown.

I lifted my gaze and met his. My heart sank as I saw his concern. Tom loved Joe. Heck, so did Scott. We would often do cookouts at my house, and the boys would hang out by the grill, chatting. This was going to break his heart too. Maybe he would even resent me?

"I'm just... I have—"

I didn't get to finish the sentence before our boss, Chief Jake Doyle, came rushing out of his office and approached us. He looked at me and Tom.

"You two will miss the meeting this morning. They are dragging a body out of the retention pond on South Brevard Avenue at Tenth Street as we speak. Brace yourselves. First responders said it was a kid."

<u>Keep reading here!</u>
https://geni.us/B0CNTVS39Wendmatter1

About the Author

Willow Rose is a multi-million-copy best-selling Author and an Amazon ALL-star Author of more than 90 novels.

Several of her books have reached the top 10 of ALL books in the Amazon store in the US, UK, and Canada.

She has sold more than six million books that are translated into many languages.

Willow's books are fast-paced, nail-biting pageturners with twists you won't see coming.

That's why her fans call her The Queen of Plot Twists.

Willow lives on Florida's Space Coast. When she is not writing or reading, you will find her surfing and watching the dolphins play in the waves of the Atlantic Ocean.

Join Willow Rose's VIP Newsletter to get exclusive updates about New Releases, Giveaways, and FREE ebooks.

Just scan this QR code with your phone and click on the link:

SCAN ME

Win a waterproof Kindle e-reader or a $125 Amazon giftcard!
Just become a member of my Facebook group **WILLOW ROSE - MYSTERY SERIES.**
Every time we pass 1000 new members, we'll randomly select a winner from all the entries.

To enter go here: https://www.facebook.com/groups/1921072668197253

Tired of too many emails? Text the word: "willowrose" to 31996 to sign up to Willow's VIP text List to get a text alert with news about New Releases, Giveaways, Bargains and Free books from Willow.

FOLLOW WILLOW ROSE ON BOOKBUB HERE: HTTPS://WWW.BOOKBUB.COM/AUTHORS/WILLOW-ROSE

Follow Willow on BookBub

Connect with Willow online:
https://www.facebook.com/willowredrose
https://twitter.com/madamwillowrose
http://www.goodreads.com/author/show/4804769.Willow_Rose
https://www.willow-rose.net
Mail to: contact@willow-rose.net

f facebook.com/willowredrose
X x.com/madamwillowrose
O instagram.com/madamewillowrose

Books by the Author

HARRY HUNTER MYSTERY SERIES

- ALL THE GOOD GIRLS
- RUN GIRL RUN
- NO OTHER WAY
- NEVER WALK ALONE

MARY MILLS MYSTERY SERIES

- WHAT HURTS THE MOST
- YOU CAN RUN
- YOU CAN'T HIDE
- CAREFUL LITTLE EYES

EVA RAE THOMAS MYSTERY SERIES

- SO WE LIE
- DON'T LIE TO ME
- WHAT YOU DID
- NEVER EVER
- SAY YOU LOVE ME
- LET ME GO
- IT'S NOT OVER
- NOT DEAD YET
- TO DIE FOR
- SUCH A GOOD GIRL
- LITTLE DID SHE KNOW
- YOU BETTER RUN

- Say It Isn't So
- Too Pretty To Die
- Till Death Do Us Part

EMMA FROST SERIES

- Itsy Bitsy Spider
- Miss Dolly had a Dolly
- Run, Run as Fast as You Can
- Cross Your Heart and Hope to Die
- Peek-a-Boo I See You
- Tweedledum and Tweedledee
- Easy as One, Two, Three
- There's No Place like Home
- Slenderman
- Where the Wild Roses Grow
- Waltzing Mathilda
- Drip Drop Dead
- Black Frost

JACK RYDER SERIES

- Hit the Road Jack
- Slip out the Back Jack
- The House that Jack Built
- Black Jack
- Girl Next Door
- Her Final Word
- Don't Tell

REBEKKA FRANCK SERIES

- One, Two...He is Coming for You

- THREE, FOUR...BETTER LOCK YOUR DOOR
- FIVE, SIX...GRAB YOUR CRUCIFIX
- SEVEN, EIGHT...GONNA STAY UP LATE
- NINE, TEN...NEVER SLEEP AGAIN
- ELEVEN, TWELVE...DIG AND DELVE
- THIRTEEN, FOURTEEN...LITTLE BOY UNSEEN
- BETTER NOT CRY
- TEN LITTLE GIRLS
- IT ENDS HERE

MYSTERY/THRILLER/HORROR NOVELS

- SORRY CAN'T SAVE YOU
- IN ONE FELL SWOOP
- UMBRELLA MAN
- BLACKBIRD FLY
- TO HELL IN A HANDBASKET
- EDWINA

HORROR SHORT-STORIES

- MOMMY DEAREST
- THE BIRD
- BETTER WATCH OUT
- EENIE, MEENIE
- ROCK-A-BYE BABY
- NIBBLE, NIBBLE, CRUNCH
- HUMPTY DUMPTY
- CHAIN LETTER

PARANORMAL SUSPENSE/ROMANCE NOVELS

- IN COLD BLOOD

- THE SURGE
- GIRL DIVIDED

THE VAMPIRES OF SHADOW HILLS SERIES

- FLESH AND BLOOD
- BLOOD AND FIRE
- FIRE AND BEAUTY
- BEAUTY AND BEASTS
- BEASTS AND MAGIC
- MAGIC AND WITCHCRAFT
- WITCHCRAFT AND WAR
- WAR AND ORDER
- ORDER AND CHAOS
- CHAOS AND COURAGE

THE AFTERLIFE SERIES

- BEYOND
- SERENITY
- ENDURANCE
- COURAGEOUS

THE WOLFBOY CHRONICLES

- A GYPSY SONG
- I AM WOLF

DAUGHTERS OF THE JAGUAR

- SAVAGE
- BROKEN

Copyright Willow Rose 2023
Published by BUOY MEDIA LLC
All rights reserved.

No part of this book may be reproduced, scanned, or distributed in any printed or electronic form without permission from the author.

This is a work of fiction. Any resemblance of characters to actual persons, living or dead is purely coincidental. The Author holds exclusive rights to this work. Unauthorized duplication is prohibited.

Cover design by Juan Villar Padron,
https://www.juanjpadron.com

Special thanks to my editor Janell Parque
http://janellparque.blogspot.com/

Printed in the USA
CPSIA information can be obtained
at www.ICGtesting.com
LVHW101547271223
767352LV00004B/301

9 781954 938458